About the author

Judith Ann Smith was born in Manchester in 1948. She studied Social Science at University followed by training as a Career Guidance Practitioner. Now retired, she lives in West Lancashire and this is her first published book.

Music, art and the natural world provided the inspiration as well as an abiding interest in human behaviour.

For Margaret
with best wishes
from Judith Ann Smith
Feb 2019

BORN IN JANUARY

Judith Ann Smith

BORN IN JANUARY

Vanguard Press

VANGUARD PAPERBACK

A CIP catalogue record for this title is
available from the British Library.

ISBN 978 1 784653 51 4

*Vanguard Press is an imprint of
Pegasus Elliot MacKenzie Publishers Ltd.*
www.pegasuspublishers.com

First Published in 2018

**Vanguard Press
Sheraton House Castle Park
Cambridge England**

Printed & Bound in Great Britain

Dedication

for Beatrix Garner

CHAPTER ONE

NAZ

Every bad thing that happened to me I blamed on having red hair. That day was no exception. The door of my father's studio had been left slightly ajar and I could see the figure of my mother, Lara, bending over the old suitcase in the corner of the room. For some reason she always called the case a portmanteau. She was holding something in both hands which looked like a photograph. A shaft of sunlight caught her chestnut hair, fading at the sides but still thick and glossy despite her advancing years. I paused to admire her profile, more handsome than pretty, and the way she could fold her long, ample body into an elegant squat. She was wearing a mustard yellow dress which suited her well. For my mother, having red hair had always seemed to be a blessing. I was about to enter the room when I heard her speak in a whisper. At first I imagined she had a mobile phone, but no, she was speaking to the photograph. How strange, I thought. I strained to hear, conscious of prying but curious about my mother's uncharacteristic behaviour.

The words sounded like, "Jake... I love you still," but I wasn't sure. She looked around the empty room almost furtively and then she began to sob quietly. Eventually, she spoke again very softly. "I've been longing to tell you this. You are the father of my three children."

Stunned and puzzled by what I had heard, I leaned against the grey wall opposite the studio until the shock waves had passed. I found the coolness of the wall on my back surprisingly comforting. I remember I was wearing a good blue check shirt bought in Jermyn Street and I was aware of wet patches under my arms. I made a mental note to have a shower later, which was curious given the scene I had just witnessed. It was a scene which disturbed me greatly. I turned round and began to descend as quietly as I could, but one of the stairs creaked so I ran down on tiptoe, not wishing to be found eavesdropping. I came across our cat, Jasmin, on its way up, and I almost threw it to the top as a distraction for my mother.

I was alarmed to hear Mother call my name. "Naz, love, is that you?" She waited, then said, "Oh, it's you Jasmin. You naughty cat startling me like that." I could imagine her scooping up the cat, and holding her close, the cat purring with pleasure.

When I reached the bottom I was trembling and that familiar feeling of childhood insecurity began to surface. I took a few deep breaths and went to the kitchen to brew some strong Italian coffee. I was struggling to stop my hands from shaking. What I had overheard seemed unreal and in a way trivial, and yet for me it was one of those life changing moments and my mind was in turmoil. I had been upstairs in search of my mother to share my good news but now everything I depended on had been shattered in those few moments.

Many thoughts raced through my head. My father, now dead, was called Jack, and I had a twin brother,

Josh. My brother and I are like chalk and cheese. People say we look alike but he is a bit smaller and carries more weight and is better looking, I think. I was born about twenty minutes after him and straight away adopted the younger brother role. I know I am bold and ambitious in my job, but when it comes to everyday situations I tend to hang back whilst he is always confident and happy to lead. Josh would have confronted mother and not ran away. I idolised him and he looked after me whenever there was trouble. Nevertheless, I grew up with a feeling that there was something missing in my life and this caused me great anxiety in my teenage years. A strange sense of loss followed me into adulthood, and my mother's words in the studio prompted similar emotions.

The aroma of fresh coffee calmed me down, and as I sipped my drink I felt in a better frame of mind and started to wonder if I had misheard my mother. I was sure my brother Josh would say this was the case, and that my imagination had been working overtime as usual. Even so, there was a niggling doubt in the back of my mind and I knew I needed to establish the truth somehow. Firstly, I must check out the photograph in the suitcase, then maybe my mind would be at rest. This simple act was not going to be so straightforward. Since childhood the studio had been out of bounds because of my father working there. For some reason, we had continued to obey that even after his death, partly as a mark of respect but also because we had both left home and it seemed a bit intrusive to go sneaking around the house.

I was conscious that my vivid imagination often transported me into worlds purely of my own design.

Whilst this was helpful in my job as a landscape architect, it could often be misleading in daily life. My reverie was interrupted by the noise of my mother coming downstairs. She pushed open the door of the front room and I felt a lurch in my stomach as she entered.

"Hello, Naz, love. Have you been here long? I thought I heard you upstairs."

"Oh, hi Mum. No, I've just arrived. You weren't here so I made some coffee. Hope that's ok. I thought you might have popped next door."

My mother came over and bent down to hug me. Her skin was warm and soft and I was aware of her scent with its distinctive honeysuckle fragrance. I wanted to pull her close and push her away at the same time.

"I was in the attic sorting out some papers. Anyway, enough of that. Come on, tell me your news. I don't usually have the pleasure of your company on a weekday."

Somehow, the good news I wanted to share had faded into insignificance during the last twenty minutes. I took off my glasses to clean them and used the time to suspend my negative emotions and try to focus on the reason I had called.

"Shall I get you some coffee, then we can settle down and talk?"

"Thanks love. Yes, I'd like that."

She kicked off her shoes and jumped onto the sofa, curling her long legs underneath her. Jasmin appeared from nowhere and leaped onto her lap. They both looked very content and my mother's tears seemed to be long forgotten. I fetched the coffee and noticed my hand trembled a little when I passed it to her.

"Thanks love," she said, then I had her full attention.

"You remember I entered my CJ design for the British Landscapes Association competition? Well, believe it or not, I won first prize!"

"Naz, that's amazing. I am so proud of you." Mum was beaming and there were latent tears sparkling in her eyes.

"What do you win? Is it a money prize?" she said, ever practical.

"No, it's not money I'm afraid. The prize is a landscaping contract with Greenglobe Architectural Landscape Company. Remember, they did the work for the local Motune Park project. That was an amazing idea. Together with local residents, they transformed derelict buildings and neglected areas into cultural hubs. Did you ever go to see it? It had a really positive effect on the community. Before that, there'd been a lot of trouble caused by racial tension and crime, and the project seemed to give people hope. This is a one off opportunity but it could lead to more work if it goes well. Anyway, I'm really pleased about it and it will be brilliant being able to do my own thing for a change." As I spoke, my enthusiasm temporarily obscured my previous distress.

"Oh Naz, you really do deserve it. You've worked so hard and to me your designs are always unique and so beautiful... have you told Josh yet?"

"No, not yet," I replied. "I wanted you to be the first to know." This wasn't entirely true, and she probably knew this. I was the landscape designer for

Josh's architectural practice so there were some short term implications for our work relationship. I would need to discuss the practicalities with him, but I was sure he would be glad for me. I'd always clung to Josh, but at thirty-six it was time for me to stand on my own two feet. I also needed to decide whether or not to tell Josh what I had overheard in the studio.

I left my mother's house shortly after this and, as I drove home in the pink dusk, I recreated once more the scene in the studio and realised how little I knew of my mother's past.I wondered if I might have to reconcile myself to the fact that she had a secret life before us.

CHAPTER TWO

LARA

The portmanteau stood in an awkward corner of the attic. This was not an ordinary suitcase but a large, battered leather travelling bag that was hinged in the middle and opened flat. It had accompanied me and my cello far and wide but now lay redundant and bulging with memorabilia. Somewhere within was a photograph I desperately wanted to find. I would never have dreamed that the finding of the photograph would have such catastophic consequences. As I crouched over the bag I mouthed the word "portmanteau" and considered how I liked the word because it had two meanings, the other meaning being more modern and referring to a combination of two words making a new word, such as "smoke" and "fog" making "smog". I was amused by some of these combinations and had enjoyed making up ridiculous ones to entertain my sons when they were younger.

The room in which the portmanteau stood I called the attic because it was the uppermost room in the house. It was under the eaves and was unusual in shape, with exposed rafters. Prior to my husband's death we had called it "the studio" and he had added a huge skylight which gave him the north light from above, perfect for painting. He had kept one wall blank so that he could display "work in progress". We had done little else to our 1920's terraced home.

As I bent over the portmanteau, searching for the photograph, I was reminded of when I first met Jack, my husband to be. I was a student cellist at the Royal Music College and had travelled with my portmanteau to play in a concert at Cadogan Hall, famous for its impressive Art Deco interior as well as some wonderful music events.

"Do you mind if I monopolise you for the evening?" were the first words he said to me.

I thought it a rather quaint opening line at the time, given that it was the late sixties. I had gone on to a post-concert party in a flat near the Kings Road in Chelsea, and there he was. Apparently he had attended the concert although he wasn't a great lover of classical music, and I realized later that he was probably drawn to the building for its architecture, rather than to listen to a very plain young cellist.

I was a bit hesitant about responding to his question but in the end replied, "Fine, but I hope you don't regret it."

I was never sure why I said this but it seemed to have the desired effect, as we smooched the night away to Bob Dylan in the marijuana smoke-filled room whilst everyone else relaxed on big cushions. The joyous final movement of Hadyn's cello concerto in C was still in my consciousness, and the combination was strange but magical. I was tempted to play the notes up and down his warm back but resisted. I cringe to think of it now.

I had changed from my long black concert gown into a very short number, mini dresses being all the rage of course, and had pulled on some long boots which made me look even taller than my normal five foot eight. Jack wore blue jeans, a white T shirt and a black leather jacket. His dark blonde hair was collar length. I wasn't really up to date with men's fashion in the sixties so I was unsure whether he was a mod, a rocker or a hippy. Maybe he was just timeless. He had the physique of a rugby forward but it was his eyes that attracted me. They were the sort of blue that changes with the light, at times quite pale and then suddenly, deep sapphire. His accent was cultured and he was unmistakably from the North East. Durham was his home town, it turned out, so at least I could place him.

"I'm Jack Greenhill," he had said, by way of introduction.

"Oh, my name's Larayne. Larayne Ackroyd. My friends call me Lara."

"Could I be counted amongst your friends?"

"Maybe. Yes, I think so," I laughed.

"In that case, I'm delighted to meet you, Lara."

His old world courtesy beguiled me, especially when combined with Geordie, as it sometimes was. When I asked him what he did, he said, "Have a guess. What would you like me to be... an investment banker or maybe a dentist?"

I must have looked surprised or impressed, as he followed this with, "To tell you the truth, pet, I'm a post grad student at Glasgow Art College. I'm researching the influences of the Art Deco movement on advertising, particularly the work of Cassandre." He paused to see if his words had had the desired effect. "Have you heard of Cassandre?"

I shook my head, wondering what was going to come next.

"No, not many people have, but he's well known in my field."

At this point he led me to a plump sofa and invited me to sit down. Jack then regaled me with a mini lecture on his subject.

"I know so much about Cassandre that I almost feel he's an old friend. He was born in 1901 and he's still alive today. He's one of the greatest poster designers of the twentieth century, I believe. He was born in the Ukraine and his real name is Adolphe Mouron, but his family had to flee to Paris because of the hostile political climate." Jack paused for breath. "Shall I go on?"

I nodded politely, doing my best to concentrate, although it was quite hard going. Having said that, I was full of admiration for his knowledge and passion and he reminded me of myself when I talked about my music.

"He studied painting at one of the Paris colleges, but when he was about twenty-two he started to design posters using the name Cassandre."

"What sort of posters did he design?" I asked, struggling to think of something intelligent to say as art was not my forte. By now I was more focussed on Jack rather than his words. His face was relaxed yet animated and a smile played around his mouth. His blue eyes captivated me, as did his soft, clear voice and slender long fingered hands, the hands of an artist, with which he gestured continually.

"His style is typically Art Deco and his posters became iconic images of the 1920s and 30s."

"How would you describe Art Deco to an ignoramus like me? I think I can recognize Art Deco architecture, like this lovely building, but that's about it."

"Well, have you got a few weeks? No of course not... so briefly, Art Deco is a fusion of various twentieth century styles, a combination of Art Nouveau's stylized curves and the geometric abstraction of Cubism, Futurism and Constructivism." He stopped to smile at me, then continued, "Cassandre's style greatly influenced advertising art in the early twentieth century, and his posters celebrate the luxurious transport and modern machine technology of his day. You really need to look at some of these to get what I mean. Is that enough?" Jack laughed again, clearly aware that I was overwhelmed.

"So, in other words, you came to the concert and turned up at the party for the Art Deco interest, and not because of me?" I teased.

He laughed and this marked the start of our relationship. At midnight I had to do my Cinderella act, as I had a train to catch in the morning to my next concert venue.

"Can I offer you a lift home?" he said. I remember thinking how charming he was.

"Well, no thanks. That's very kind, but I was going to walk. The hotel's only a few roads away," I said, feeling a little agitated. I wasn't keen to extend the evening as I had to rise very early the next day. But he looked so crestfallen that I relented.

"Good. You'll need these," he said, passing me a motorcycle helmet and a thick, bright yellow sweater which had been concealed in a rucksack by the door.

I immediately regretted giving in, but had no choice but to clamber on the back of his Triton bike, conscious that I had a lot of leg showing. When I discovered later that Triton is a portmanteau word derived from the contraction of two brands, Triumph and Norton, I considered this a good omen.

When I think back to that time, I realise the saga that follows is not primarily a romantic tale, despite its beginnings, but a story of people appearing, disappearing and reappearing, and the complications which arise. Indeed, Jack delivered me to my hotel with no promises for the future and then disappeared not just for weeks but for several years. I had no contact number and we had not shared a lot of information, so where he lived was a mystery to me. I moved on, as we say these days.

It is also a story about place and connection. Places where people arrive, live, leave and visit, and the serendipitous connections between people and places.

Out of the blue, Jack phoned me six years later. It was March 23rd 1974 and my birthday. I was due at my party that evening, accompanied by Jake, my current admirer and was astonished that Jack had tracked me down after such a long absence and had chosen this day to get in touch. He always maintained that he wasn't aware of my birthday, which confirmed my belief that our lives would remain entwined in some way.

The phone rang just as I was dressing. My silky gold dress hung ready on the back of the bedroom door. It had net sleeves and a low back and had last been worn by me at my best friend's wedding. My stockings were pale in colour and I was wearing old fashioned, but comfortable, black patent leather stilettos. I had let my hair uncoil and had brushed it one hundred times so that it hung down my back like a polished, bronze mirror.

"Hello," Jack said. "How's the cello? And how's Jacqueline Du Pre? I believe her new Elgar Cello Concerto recording is well worth a listen!"

I recognized his voice immediately. I hesitated in replying but strangely, I remember feeling completely at ease with him.

"Oh, hello! What a lovely surprise. I've been wondering how you are and where you've been hiding... did you finish your Cassandre project?" He had acknowledged my interests and I wanted to return the compliment.

"Slow down, pet. What a lot of questions! Why don't we meet for a drink and I can update you about my adventures?"

"Yes, yes. I'd like that. When are you free?"

"Well, what about this evening? About eight at the Bull and Dog?"

"Oh, sorry. I'm out this evening at a birthday party."

"Shame. Do you have to go? Whose party is it?"

"It's mine actually. I'm twenty-six today."

"Then I suppose you have to go." He waited, possibly hoping I'd issue an invitation. But of course, I couldn't.

"Would your social calendar allow you to come tomorrow, or are you flying to Paris? Or worse still, are you married?" he said mischievously.

"I've no concert or rehearsals and I'm not married, so that would be fine."

"Excellent. See you then." With that he rang off.

I quelled a vague sense of anticipation and continued dressing as if nothing had occurred.

After my party, I told Jake that I was meeting an old friend for a drink the next evening. I remember a sort of shadow flickered over his face, then he smiled.

He had a way of gazing at me as if looking into my soul. It could be quite disconcerting.

Anyway, he said, "Good. Well I hope you have a lovely catch up. I'll call you sometime next week."

He kissed me passionately as always then drove off at great speed in his dark red XR7.

We had shared much ardour and many adventures, but that was the last time I saw him for several months. I accepted this without regret as that was the nature of our relationship.

I had no guilty conscience about pursuing a romance with Jack, and the next time I saw Jake, Jack and I were about to be married. The one thing I did regret was that their names were so similar and I was sure this might lead to confusion at some point in the future.

CHAPTER THREE

LARA

As arranged, I met Jack at eight the next evening at the Bull and Dog in Belgravia. The pub was quite difficult to find, tucked away in a quiet mews. I'd heard of the pub because of its connections with celebrities but had never been inside. I have to say, it seemed quite traditional and ordinary but there was an open fire, old fashioned furniture and a welcoming atmosphere. It seemed a good place to sit and watch the world go by.

The pub was very busy but I spotted Jack at a table near the window and was glad he'd arrived before me. I noticed a lot of punks, a few with safety pins in their noses as well as ear jewellery, and the general dress code was ripped jeans, torn tee shirts and scrappy dyed hair. It was a different world from the one I normally inhabited, but it excited me.

"Hello Jack," I said.

He jumped up and greeted me with a hug. I could smell freshly washed hair but he didn't look as if he'd shaved recently. His crisp shirt was pale blue and he wore a grey sleeveless pullover that looked like fine cashmere.

"Lara, good to see you... sit down and I'll get you a drink. What would you like?"

I took off my coat to reveal my outfit, a white blouse, pale pink cardigan and black maxi skirt with short lace up boots. I clutched my coat for a while, feeling a little nervous but laid it on the chair next to me. When Jack returned with my Bacardi and Coke, and his pint of Fuller's ale. I thought I detected a look of appreciation, certainly a warm smile, and I soon relaxed.

"Interesting pub," I said.

"Yes, it has quite a history. I'm sure you know?"

"Well, I know various rock stars and actors used the pub in the sixties, but I'm not sure who."

"Yes, apparently it was a favourite haunt of the rich and famous, as well as a hangout for London's master criminals. There are even stories of villains using the pub to plot bank raids and diamond thefts. In the fifties and sixties the criminals quaffed champagne alongside famous film stars."

We both laughed at the thought of this.

Jack had a way of leaning back with legs outstretched and arms clasped behind his head when he was in full flow. He became very demonstrative and his north east accent was more pronounced.

At this stage in our relationship I was beguiled by his ability to recall and share information, but later it sometimes felt as if he was opinionated and wanted to be the centre of attention. After a second drink I remember our conversation moved on to talking about our different lives. Jack asked me where I came from originally and about my family, so I gave him a potted version.

"I grew up in a village in West Yorkshire on the edge of the Pennines. We lived on a post war council estate, my mum worked in a sewing factory and my dad was a miner until last year. The pit closed, so he's a long distance lorry driver now. That's about it!"

Jack listened intently and almost with disbelief.

"Is this all true?" he said.

"Yes, of course. Why do you ask?"

"Well, you seem so refined. From your accent I thought you came from south of Watford!" I must have looked aggrieved as he then apologised profusely and said, "Sorry. I must sound really snobbish. I think it's brilliant you've done so well. Your parents must be amazing to have encouraged and supported you."

"You're right. I've got the best parents in the world. They sacrificed a lot to let me go to music college." I thought Jack's tone rather condescending but decided to forgive him as he seemed genuinely interested in my life story.

"How did you first discover you wanted to play the cello?" He said.

"Oh, my dad was musical. He played trumpet in the colliery band and we always had the Third Programme playing on the radio. I went to the Girls' Grammar School and my music teacher, Mr Presley, we called him Elvis of course, seemed to think I had some talent so it took off from there. I went to a few classical concerts and the cello always enchanted me so I was thrilled when school arranged for me to borrow one, and they found a pot of money to pay for my lessons. After my A levels I won a place at the Royal Music College to train as a professional cellist."

I will never forget what happened next. There was a masive explosion which shook the walls of the pub. Everyone was stunned into silence and then there was talking in hushed tones. We were all uncertain about how to react. I looked across at Jack and he took my hand gently. I was conscious that my whole body was shaking.

"Don't worry Lara, I'm sure it's nothing serious. I'll go and take a look outside."

"Please be careful, Jack. It sounded like a bomb to me." I wasn't being melodramatic as there had been several car bomb incidents recently in the city.

Jack squeezed my shoulder before he departed and gave me a reassuring smile, though his brow was furrowed. As he moved towards the door other men began to join him but just at that moment a policeman entered.

"We need to evacuate the pub," he said. "A car bomb has gone off opposite and there may be others. Please start to leave in an orderly fashion."

He sounded very calm and his manner was kind as he ushered us all outside.

I clung on to Jack's arm and soon we were on the pavement. We were hit by a huge cloud of smoke and there was a commotion with lots of people wandering around aimlessly. Some seemed to be nursing cuts on their faces and arms. Others were sobbing quietly. The blast from the bomb had ruptured a water main so that there was a small flood of about two feet deep covering the road.

The car was in flames and appeared to be a massive fireball. Windows in shop fronts nearby had shattered and there was a pungent smell which Jack said was gunpowder. The police were shouting to everyone to move back as there could be another bomb.

"I'll see if I can speak to someone, to check if we can leave. You'd probably like to get home."

"Oh, yes please," I said. I still felt shaky and wanted to escape from the scene. "Can you check if anyone has been hurt?" The terror was so great I felt like running but knew that I mustn't.

"Yes, I'll do that." Jack gave the impression he was very controlled but he admitted later that he was scared too.

When Jack returned he said, "The car was parked opposite the pub and the police received a warning by phone. They attempted to clear the area and were about to evacuate the pub when the bomb went off. There was no one in the car, thankfully. A few bystanders were hurt but nothing serious, mainly cuts to different parts of their bodies. But everyone seems to be in shock."

"Is it OK to go home now?" I said, probably sounding rather helpless.

"Yes, they said that's fine. I'll take you back. Here, do you want to take my arm? It's all been a bit traumatic, hasn't it?"

I was grateful and linked my arm through his, whilst we walked the half mile to my rented house. I was relieved there was no motorbike on this occasion.

On the news the next day we learned that the Prime Minister had been recalled from holiday. The IRA was believed to be responsible at a time when the peace process was in jeopardy.

CHAPTER FOUR

JAKE

Lara was the love of my life even though she wasn't a Jewish girl. When I talk about love I refer, of course, to my enduring and extreme passion for her body. Our conversations were generally inconsequential but our love making was like floating on a heavenly planet— Venus, naturally. I could describe this in scientific terms but perhaps not. I first noticed Lara in the bookshop in town. How could I miss her? She was about six feet tall (I jest) and had long, slim legs, a narrow body and square shoulders. Strangely, her facial features, though appealing individually, were curiously asymmetrical when combined, and created a rather plain countenance. She was in the music section and I had been browsing Sci-fi. I positioned myself next to her and when she accidentally knocked over a large pile of books, which had been perched precariously on the table, I leapt forward to assist.

"Oh, thanks," she said, only glancing in my direction.

She clearly wasn't embarrassed, as if she made a habit of causing chaos. I bent down to gather up some of the books and together we replaced them in a tall pile back on the table. She then carried on with her book search.

"Are you looking for anything in particular?" I enquired.

She turned towards me and almost disdainfully replied, "Yes, it's a work called *The Music Theory. Handbook for cello students*."

"Ah, you're a music student."

"Good guess."

I decided things couldn't get much worse, so I took the plunge.

"I'm Jacob Newman. Jake to my friends."

At last her expression softened and she broke into a smile.

"That's my line... I usually say my name's Larayne, but my friends call me Lara."

Later, she gave me a rather fanciful explanation, telling me that one of her favourite literary figures was Larissa Fyodrovna, also known as Lara, from Boris Pasternak's book *Dr Zhivago*. I had no knowledge of the book but had seen the gorgeous Julie Christie in the film, when dragged along by a girlfriend, and that was good enough for me. So Lara she became.

Just at that moment, a small benign looking man who had occupied a high stool at the counter came over to us. I knew him well. He wore round spectacles and a black felt beret perched jauntily on his head. He also sported a little goatee beard and an amused expression played on his face.

"Are you all right, my dear?" he said, with traces of a foreign accent.

Lara turned to him and smiled. She towered above him but in character they were equal.

"Yes, I'm fine. So sorry about the books. I think we've put them back safely."

"Good. I'm glad my son has been of help to you."

Lara looked dumbfounded. Her gaze went from me to my father and back again. She was obviously trying to detect similarities in our appearances.

"I'd like to introduce my father. Father, this is my new friend Lara."

Lara and my father shook hands and then we all laughed as if sharing a good joke.

"We make excellent coffee and bagels next door. I think Jacob might like to treat you."

Lara paid for her book first and my father exclaimed with delight, "A musician! Wonderful. Wonderful. If only my son had studied music the world would be a better place. What use is astrophysics?"

He shrugged his shoulders and clapped his hands as if to congratulate himself. We all laughed again.

Over fresh bagels, apple cake and strong coffee Lara and I got to know each other. After that, we started to meet for a meal somewhere quite ordinary like the Taj Mahal or Lee's. The restaurants would be full of cigarette smoke and we occasionally indulged ourselves with a Gitanne and a glass of Mateus Rose. Then we would drift back to my flat for the evening.

When we met it was the late sixties. She was eighteen and a cello student at the Royal Music College. I had finished my PhD in astrophysics and was working as a researcher attached to the Astronomy Department of the university in the south of the city. My job took me to many different places, so relationships with women were invariably superficial. Lara's interest in my work was feigned, I'm sure, but I tried to answer her questions in a simple way.

"Why did you choose a difficult subject astrophysics?"

"Well... I've always been interested in the big questions in life like how we can reach other planets, how the human body adapts to new places, how the planets were formed and what are the unique conditions that give rise to life. Basically, I'm nosy and I enjoy problem solving. Shall I go on?"

"No." She laughed, "I think I get it. I love the stars so that's a start."

We never had a similar conversation about her music but she didn't seem to mind.

A week after I met Lara we made love, the first time for her, in my bedroom. I lived in what would now be described as an apartment on the third floor of a large Victorian house. The house had bay windows, iron railings around the front, patterned Flemish brickwork and stained glass in the doors and windows, through which the sun made rainbow prisms. There were sash windows at the back and Lara often looked out from the bedroom to see the acre of garden below, with its terraced lawns, shrubbery, an orchard of cox orange pippins, an outdoor seating area and a stable for storage of bikes and other stuff. Friends seemed to think the sitting room was elegant with its interesting proportions and ornamental detail. I remember the colour scheme was dominated by rich burgundy, green and blue. There was an attractive cast iron fireplace and the room was crammed with furniture, including two overstuffed settees and a battered purple chaise longue. In the kitchen there was a huge wooden table polished with age, and also a walk-in larder, which was useful. The floors were old pine covered with dark threadbare carpets. To reach my flat we had to climb a long staircase with elaborate twisted balustrades. Lara was fascinated by these and always ran her fingers along them as she climbed. My personal taste was much more contemporary, but I could appreciate the solid Victorian character of my rooms.

Lara and I shared no interests and I'm not sure we particularly liked each other except in bed. She could be rather headstrong and self-centred and I'm sure she found me stubborn and intolerant at times. Later on, our rendezvous were clandestine as we both had formed casual relationships with other people. Occasionally, we met abroad, and during our last memorable summer she came to visit me in Tenerife where I was on secondment for a few months with a renowned observatory.

I recognised Lara at once in the airport crowd, with her chestnut hair, towering above the rest. When she came closer I was once more struck by the incongruity of her features, but her smile made me glad she had come. We embraced and I caught the scent of her perfume, reminding me of honeysuckle. I took some leave and we stayed in cheap boarding houses pretending to be husband and wife.

I always think of Tenerife as the island of joy. In the sixties the island found prosperity largely due to the tourism driven property boom. Lara and I escaped the crowds and spent most of our time in a tranquil and gracious town called Garachio. It was a place flanked by fragrant forested slopes and a rocky coastline. The houses were whitewashed and the streets narrow and cobbled. We found a room in a sixteenth century manor house centred around a courtyard, with a fountain in the middle. The floors were made of cherry wood and the décor was muted, with Mediterranean blue tiles in the bathroom. The bed was very large, cool and welcoming and the linen smelled of lavender.

We passed the days swimming in the volcanic caves and lying together on the rocks. At night we ate tapas, chorizo, omelettes and manchego cheese washed down with beer or sangria. During this time we seemed to grow closer and I came to respect Lara more. She was happy to wander off by herself to explore and had an open friendliness with everyone she met. Her schoolgirl Spanish was enough to start a conversation. But she could also be aloof and tactless, like the way she always ignored the girl who brought our drinks and continued to talk. She also frequently ignored me when I was speaking and carried on reading her cello score. However, if I admired an attractive girl, I got Lara's attention immediately and she would overreact and become quite petulant. A lot of the time I think her mind was filled with music and there was little room for anything else.

It was our last afternoon together and we lay on the bed, my arm around her, luxuriating in the warm light filtering through the shutters. I remember she sighed softly and turned to look at me. I had a sense that something unusual was about to happen, like when a comet passes close to the sun and we wait to see if it survives.

"I do love you," she whispered.

I hesitated then replied, "I guess I feel the same."

We both knew that this love was born of the moment and would vanish as quickly as it had appeared. Even so, when she caught her train to the airport she was in tears and I was sad to see her go.

I returned home a month later, and not long after, I received a phone call from Lara inviting me to her birthday party. She was twenty-six and I could hardly believe we had known each other for such a long time. I had nothing planned so I said I would go if I could be her escort for the evening. She seemed pleased.

After the party, when we were saying goodbye, Lara said, "I'm seeing an old friend for a drink tomorrow. He's just come back from a tour of Italy."

"Great. Well I hope you have a lovely catch up. I'll call you next week."

I felt relieved, in a way, as I had met a gorgeous Jewish girl at a friend's party and wanted to ask her out. After this, I recall I sped off in my TR7 and didn't see Lara again for about a year.

CHAPTER FIVE

JACK

I will never forget that day in April 1974 when an IRA car bomb exploded outside the pub where Lara and I had met after six years apart. After the incident, I offered to take Lara home, of course, as she seemed very shaken by the experience. To tell the truth I was quite disturbed by it myself and glad to have Lara's company. We walked the half mile to where she lived. She hung onto my arm and didn't speak but hummed a tune which I think was a cello piece. I couldn't put a name to it, but she told me later it was from Dvorak's cello concerto in B. This may have been her way of coping.

We reached the front door of her house. It was an early nineteenth century property which she shared with a friend from the orchestra. I discovered that the house was quite small with a bedroom on each floor. The kitchen was in the basement, and the tiny front parlour had a rustic looking bay window. Her bedroom had a balcony with views of "the rooftops". One of the upstairs rooms accommodated her cello and there were books and flowers everywhere, all higgledy-piggledy.

I was about to press the doorbell when I felt her go limp. There were beads of perspiration on her brow and her hand was very clammy. Her skin, which was always pale, had become a translucent greenish white colour and there were red tinges on her cheeks. As she fainted I managed to catch her and lifted her up into my arms. The scent of her body reminded me of honeysuckle.

With difficulty I rang the doorbell and waited. The door opened and a small, dark haired young woman was standing there. I remember she had a pile of glossy back combed hair arranged in what I believe was called a bouffant style, and she wore a short red kaftan type of garment, with bare legs and feet. Her toenails were painted the colour of scarlet, clashing with her dress, but somehow appealing. The girl's expression was lively but surprised.

"Oh my goodness," she said. Her accent was southern and I learned later she was from Brighton.

"Whatever's happened lovie? Come in, come in."

I explained about the bomb and the girl ushered me in and suggested I take Lara upstairs to her room. "I'll bring you both a nice cup of tea. Plenty of sugar. That should do the trick. I'm Felice, by the way. What's your name? Jack? That's nice." Then she disappeared.

Lara's room was quite dark with the curtains half drawn, so much so that it was only later I noticed the Cassandre poster print on the wall. It was the advertising poster for the Nord Express, which had been designed by Adolphe Mouron Cassandre in 1927. It showed a stylised image of a train speeding towards the horizon with a cloud of smoke and the blue sky above. It was meant to convey the glamour of travel in that era. I was impressed and touched to see it there.

I laid Lara gently on the bed and soon she opened her eyes. "Jack! What are you doing here?"She smiled and I sensed her vulnerability waning and her confidence returning. I was seated on a chair at a respectable distance from her bed and stretched over to touch her hand. She grasped my fingertips and said, "Thank you for coming back after all this time..."

Just at that point, Felice knocked on the door and appeared with two mugs of tea and some bourbon biscuits.

"Lara, love, you're looking better. How do you feel?" She came over to the bed and looked intently at Lara. She gave her a kiss on the cheek and then disappeared again. The tea was heavily sugared but lifted our spirits.

Lara was stretched out on the mahogany bed, her head resting on a pristine white pillow. I couldn't decide whether she brought to mind a Modigliani painting or a Picasso with her long narrow face and uneven features. Yet her tangle of bronze curls (for she had changed her hairstyle since first we met) was more in keeping with a Pre-Raphaelite work. Her complexion was once more pale peach with faint freckles covering her long nose. I decided then that I had to paint her and wanted her to pose with her cello.

"Could you leave me now? I'm feeling a bit washed out," she said.

"On one condition," I replied. "That I call in tomorrow to check you're ok."

"No, sorry. I've got a rehearsal most of the day and I'll need to do a bit more practice in the evening. We're performing on Saturday and it's a difficult piece."

"OK. When would be convenient for madam?" I said, trying not to sound too dejected.

"Sunday would be good. What about brunch? I'll cook if you like."

I was astonished at the invitation but glad that Lara felt relaxed enough to issue it.

"Brilliant! But please don't go to any trouble."

"Don't worry, I won't! It'll probably be spag bol with a bottle of plonk."

"The plonk sounds good, I'll bring a bottle, and so does the spag, but I don't eat meat, so...."

"Oh!" she said, obviously surprised. "How did you get so big on vegetables?"

I laughed and told her that I'd arrive early, and show her how to create a mouth-watering vegetarian sauce with fresh pasta. I assured her she wouldn't lose weight on this diet.

As I walked to the tube station my heart lifted, for the first time in many months. The death of my father over a year ago had overwhelmed me, so much so that I had left my lecturing job at the art college and escaped to Europe on my motorbike. To be honest, even after a few years I had begun to feel greatly inhibited by college politics and having to conform to the requirements of art course curricula. I always felt more at ease being in control of my situation. So resigning, in itself, did not distress me. It would have happened sooner or later.

My travels took me, eventually, to Italy where I settled for a while in Perugia. I found it to be an attractive hill town with a strong tradition of culture and art and I soon felt at home. It was there that I re-discovered my love of drawing and painting and I realised that this was where my ambitions lay. My father had left me a considerable sum of money, so for the time being I didn't need to worry about surviving.

When I returned to London in 1973 I rented a flat in Camden Town and some studio space at the Lock Market. I used to start work when the light was right, usually a couple of hours after sunrise, and if I was up early enough I would walk in the park before that and buy a bagel and coffee from a kiosk for breakfast. This was how I found Lara again. During my lowest ebb, I had allowed no feelings to affect me apart from deep sorrow, but when I saw her in the park it was like a rainbow appearing after a storm. First of all I spotted her cello case leaning against the railings by the park lake. Then I saw her standing by a willow tree, throwing bread to the ducks. I felt such an unexpected surge of emotion that I did not dare approach her. Instead I hid behind a huge oak tree and watched. When she picked up her case and moved on I followed her at a safe distance.

She walked slowly and gracefully, almost like a giraffe, and managed her cello case with ease. At the main road she joined a long bus queue and I joined it too some way behind, eventually jumping on the same bus. I had no idea where she was going or why I was in pursuit, but I knew it was my destiny. A few stops later she alighted and I realised she was heading for Wigmore Hall.

I followed her in and stood outside the door to the hall and watched Lara hurrying to where most of the orchestra musicians were already tuning up. There was a polite cheer as she joined them and I heard her laugh. Soon they were in full flow and at this point I gave up the chase, realising that I knew how to find her now if I so wished. That was how I came to make that phone call on her birthday and how we became reunited.

CHAPTER SIX

LARA

It was Sunday and I awoke late. The previous evening had gone well and we gave two encores, so after a few relaxing glasses of wine with Felice I went to bed at midnight and slept soundly. I lay back on my pillows and enjoyed the morning light filtering through the half-open velvet curtains. Next moment, Felice bounced in with a mug of tea.

"Hey, sleepy head time to get up!" With this she reached under the eiderdown and pulled my feet.

"Get off! Leave me be. Sunday is my day of rest," I shouted.

"Not today, sweetheart. Guess who's coming for lunch?"

"Oh no!" I sighed. I'd completely forgotten my invitation to Jack and wished I'd not been so generous. But once I started to drink my tea I began to feel quite pleased with the idea and soon got myself out of bed.

I hadn't really mentioned a time for Jack to arrive so I decided to enjoy my cello practice for a while. When he appeared at eleven thirty I was still dressed in lilac shortie pyjamas, a flimsy dressing gown and suede house boots. I hadn't heard the doorbell, engrossed as I was in Bach's cello suite number one, so Felice let him in. Jack pushed open the door of the music room and stood there, looking at first amused, and then more serious. I continued to play, enjoying the resonance of the melodic music and finding the flow of sound uplifting yet peaceful.

"I must paint you just like that," he said. "Don't move whilst I do a quick sketch."

I was lost for words and did as he asked, maintaining my position, bow poised and legs inelegant astride the cello.

He dropped a big bag on the floor and some huge tomatoes and onions spilled out. Then he felt deep into the large pocket of his camel coloured duffle coat and drew out a small pad and pencil. The sketch took about fifteen minutes to complete.

"Is that it?" I said, amazed that he could produce a work of art so speedily.

"That's it for now, until you do a proper sitting for me. I'll need you to come to the studio to get the light right... Am I a bit early? I tend to get up early to work. I like the morning light," he said.

"Does that mean you'll need me at the crack of dawn for my sitting?" I joked.

Jack laughed and then began to pick up the food he had dropped.

"You seem to have a big bag of stuff to cook. Would you like some coffee before I show you the kitchen? I should probably put on some clothes, as well!"

"Coffee would be good, but don't worry about getting dressed on my account. You look fine as you are."

It was a completely innocent remark and I trusted him absolutely.

"Right. Well, come and make yourself at home, and I'll brew some coffee. Is instant OK?"

"I'll make do on this occasion pet but I'll have to show you where to get the finest coffee beans in London that don't cost the earth."

"I'll look forward to that." I could feel a grin spreading over my face and I'm not sure why but I had an uncontrollable desire to giggle. Maybe it was the unusual situation, me in my pyjamas with my cello, Jack so smart with his big bag of food, and this earnest conversation about coffee beans.

Over coffee we resumed the conversation which we had begun in the pub before that horrific incident with the bomb.

I was curious to know where Jack had disappeared over the past few years.

"Well... it's a long story," he started.

"After we met, I finished my Cassandre project and returned to Glasgow. I was offered a lectureship, which I accepted, as it gave me some security whilst I was deciding what I really wanted to do. I knew I didn't want to spend the rest of my life in an academic setting."

"You never tried to contact me, did you?" I said. "Not that I expected you to, of course."

"No. No I didn't. I assumed you regarded our little fling as a temporary affair and was sure you preferred to be free to pursue your blossoming career."

I wasn't certain if I detected a hint of sarcasm in Jack's voice, but decided to accept what he said at face value.

"Of course," I replied. "So what happened then?"

"Well, sadly my father died suddenly a year ago and I was pretty upset. My mother seemed to be coping well, so I took the opportunity to resign from the college and jumped on my motorbike with my art stuff and went off to tour Europe. I eventually reached Italy and decided to settle there a while."

"Oh. I'm truly sorry about your father. Was it his heart?"

"No... he was involved in a fatal car accident," he said. His voice was hesitant and he paused and looked down. Then he raised his head. I was shocked to see he seemed to be holding back tears. His eyes had faded to a lighter blue and his forehead became uncharacteristically furrowed. Already I was beginning to recognise his moods and I wondered if I was so easy to read. I decided to pour some more coffee and waited to see if he wanted to say more.

"Dad had been under considerable strain for quite a while with all the pit closures and redundancies. I guess he lost concentration when he was driving to work and skidded on a bend into a high wall. The medics said he would have died instantaneously, so I suppose that was a blessing. Otherwise he would have been severely brain damaged."

"Was your father going to be made redundant?" I said cautiously.

"No, he was the person making decisions for the company about which mines would close and who would be made redundant."

"You mean he was the boss?"

"Yes, you could say that."

I was surprised Jack had not mentioned his father's job when I had previously told him that my own father had been a miner. But I thought that this was unimportant and not the time to pursue it.

I was unsure what to say next after such an emotionally sensitive conversation, but he saved me the trouble by moving on to his adventures in Italy and seemed to have recovered his composure. It was only when I met his mother some time later that I discovered the full truth about his father's death.

"I loved Italy and met a chap who was associated with the Civitella Ranieri Foundation, which is based in a fifteenth century castle in Perugia."

"Sorry, what's the Civitella wotsit and where is Perugia? I've never been to Italy," I said.

He laughed. "Perugia is a wonderful hill town in central Italy and the Civitella is a foundation which was formed to bring together artists, writers and musicians from around the world. They have to show exceptional talent and commitment to be chosen, then they receive a six week residency to develop their work."

"Were you chosen to take part?"

"No, unfortunately not because Leon, the guy I met, was one of the foundation nominators and they have to remain anonymous to the applicants. If I'd been selected it would have been regarded as favouritism. Anyway, I travelled to Perugia with Leon and he introduced me to some friends who had a little apartment for rent close to the Etruscan walls. It was very quiet and had a lovely spare room with high ceilings, blessed by light from the north which I prefer for painting. This became my studio and I started to paint again." Jack became quiet for a few minutes, lost in thought.

"And what was Perugia like?" I asked, keen to hear more of his experiences.

"Well... it's really well preserved. The architecture hasn't changed for four hundred years. There are some interesting museums and churches as well as two universities... the presence of students makes the town a lively place, of course, and there's a thriving arts scene. And best of all, they've recently set up a brilliant jazz festival."

"Are there any good places to eat?"

"Yes there are. I used to meet up with Leon and his friends at a tiny trattoria, sometimes we just had plates of local cheeses with olive bread and a caraffe of prosecco, or maybe a capuccino. Other times we might have big tagliatelle with a vegetable ragu and artisan beer. The chocolate was heavenly as a pudding."

"Jack, you're making me really hungry. Do you fancy starting the meal while we talk?"

"I was getting carried away. But it's so good to talk to you about all this. Will Felice be joining us?"

"No, she's out this afternoon," I replied, glad now that she had offered to leave me to it with Jack.

Jack looked strangely vulnerable and I perceived darkness somewhere beyond his animated behaviour.

I led the way down the stairs to the basement kitchen.

"This is *bijou*," he said with a smile, taking in the small space. He began to empty his bag of food onto the table. I was amazed at the riot of colours of the vegetables and could smell the crusty bread and large piece of cheese which accompanied them. There was also some huge flat pasta which he told me was pappardelle.

"May I look at it all before you cook? I've never seen so much wonderful fresh food in this kitchen. If we have scrambled egg on toast we think that's a treat."

"Well, even scrambled egg can be exquisite when cooked in butter with a bit of smoked salmon and chives," he replied with a chuckle.

"Mm.... don't even recognise some of these. What's this for example?" I said, holding up a large wedge of a cheese-like substance.

"Oh, that's pecorino cheese. It's an Italian sheep's milk cheese. I'll be grating it to throw over the pasta, but do try a bit."

I accepted the invitation and found the cheese very hard, sharp tasting and salty. I'd tasted parmesan out of a packet but this was different.

"Where do you manage to find such exciting ingredients?"

"I usually shop at the Borough Market. They've been feeding Londoners since the thirteenth century, so that's good enough for me!"

I was even more hungry now, so I offered to open a bottle of valpolicelli in the hope that this would initiate some action. I need not have worried as he couldn't wait to get going. The smell of onions (or shallots as he corrected me) frying in olive oil was mouth-watering and I was fascinated by the speed with which he added garlic, fresh tomatoes, red pepper and mushrooms. He then added a splash of red wine and stirred. Next he tore some large leaves which he first held near my nose before washing them and throwing them in the pan.

"Recognise that?" Jack said.

"Not really. Is it a herb?" I was beginning to feel rather ignorant.

"Yes, it's fresh basil and goes really well in pasta sauces. So next time you make one do try it," he said, with a smile. I raised my eyebrows and smiled back, handing him a glass of wine.

"We'll leave that for about twenty minutes and we can start the pasta in ten. Ever tried making your own pasta?" he asked with a serious expression.

"Er, not often," I replied and he burst out laughing. I joined him, feeling pleased that he had included me in the cooking.

The meal was like heaven on a plate, so many rich flavours complemented by the valpolicelli. I was ravenous and ate without speaking. Jack did the same. Afterwards we went upstairs and relaxed on the sofa. I was intoxicated from the effects of the food and wine and felt like snuggling up to Jack, but he kept his distance. He was curious to know my story and what I had been doing since we last met all those years ago.

"Well, I finished my music course in 1969 then found a position with a small amateur orchestra in north London. It was great experience and brilliant for socialising as well. I made some very good friends. That's where I met Felice, she's a flautist, and we got on so well that we decided to get a place together." Jack nodded encouragingly. How different from Jacob, who had never asked me about my work in all the time I was with him.

"After that I was fortunate enough to win a place on a development course with my present orchestra. I was one of four students working with the composer in residence for a year. That was just so useful. I enjoyed every minute of it, though it was really hard work with not much time for leisure. It paid off though, because at the end of the year I was offered a job in the cello section."

"And did you progress from there?" Jack asked, obviously guessing what my answer would be. "You were playing solo when I sneaked into that rehearsal when I was tracking you down."

"Yes, I'm actually the principal cellist now, so from time to time I get to play solo. Not all the time, of course, as we welcome professional soloists for particular works."

"You mean like Jacqueline Du Pre?" he said with a glint in his eye.

"Yes, like her, but sadly she died in 1987 of multiple sclerosis." I had often thought it was a strange coincidence that my mother had also died of M.S. I didn't talk to Jack about this until later, as I found it too painful to discuss.

"Oh, I didn't know, of course, not being a great classical fan... until now!" Jack said, looking embarrassed.

I smiled then said, "This might interest you. I also play with a quartet at different venues around the city. It gives us the opportunity to experiment with the music a bit more, and we get younger audiences, which I like."

"You mean the music's more avant-garde?" he said

"You'll have to come and listen and decide for yourself," I challenged.

"I might just do that provided you do something for me."

"What would that be?" I asked, wary of what might come next. Jack could be rather demanding.

"Just play a bit of jazz.Something modern."

"Mm... I'm sure we could adapt something. Just leave it with me."

Jack then stood up and suggested we wash up. I thanked him but said I would do the washing up after he had left. He seemed relieved and said it was time for him to go as he had work to finish. I suddenly wondered if he was going to disappear once more and clung on to him when he gave me a hug.

"When will I see you again?" I said.

"Cue for a song?" he replied. "Sorry... What about popping over to my studio, then I can begin your portrait?"

This was the beginning of a couple of months of visits to Jack's studio whenever I could fit it in between practice and concerts. Mostly it had to be early morning or late afternoon, as he was obsessed with getting the light right. I was never allowed to see the painting while he worked. From time to time Jack came across and gently adjusted my posture and the tilt of my head. Sometimes he studied my face and hair closely then returned to his painting. This was the nearest we came to physical contact, though he always embraced me warmly when I was departing.

Even when the picture was almost finished and he didn't need me for sittings, he said he wanted to continue working on it. Despite my protestations he insisted on keeping it from me until he had done the finishing touches. I was so tempted to creep into his studio and lift the blue tasselled throw which covered the easel, but I felt this would be a betrayal, so I waited patiently.

CHAPTER SEVEN

LARA

It was June when my portrait was finished. I was eager to see the picture but Jack asked if I could contain my excitement for a while longer.

"Oh, do I really have to wait?" I said with disappointment.

"Well, I was wondering if you fancied a few days in Durham, then I'll unveil your picture when we come home," he replied. "I have one or two bits to do then it's finished."

I was surprised and bewildered as I didn't think our relationship was on the sort of footing which merited a trip to his family home. I didn't feel romantically attached to Jack as yet, but liked him a lot and felt really at ease with him, as with an older brother. I wondered if I was jumping to the wrong conclusion.

He could see that I was confused and helped me out by explaining that it was the annual Miners' Gala in Durham in July and he thought I might be interested in going, given that my father had been a miner.

"It's usually quite a party with some good speakers," he said coaxingly. "I wanted to go in memory of my dad. Although he was a boss, he had a lot of time for the men and the unions."

I felt I couldn't refuse when he said this, so I agreed on the condition that he showed me my picture on our return. I noticed from this point on that Jack's serious side tended to dominate, with very little of the earlier lightheartedness and teasing. I could only imagine that the death of his father accounted for this change.

Jack persuaded me that it would be easier to stay at his mother's house than try to find accommodation in Durham in the summer. Thus I packed my portmanteau once again and travelled by train with Jack to the North East feeling slightly nervous about the whole affair. It seemed strange leaving behind my cello and I was aware of how much I needed my music to keep me stable. We took a taxi from the station and travelled through rolling hills. When we arrived, I was impressed by the village, which looked as if it hadn't changed since the eighteenth century. It seemed to blend naturally with the landscape. I noticed two village greens with huge oak trees dominating, and there was a set of stocks on the larger one which brought a smile to my face. We passed a village pub called the Mitre and Crown and it looked very inviting. There was also a church, of course, which Jack informed me was mainly Norman with some nineteenth century restoration. The village seemed truly peaceful, almost lost in time. Jack said visitors sometimes stayed at the pub but apart from that the only busy time was when the village fair was held in August.

"We have a fancy dress parade, loads of music and food, games for the kids, craft stalls and of course sunshine!" Jack said with obvious pride.

Jack's mother's house was a large, rambling red brick place and one of the more modern houses, being built at the beginning of the twentieth century. It felt like a rustic retreat with its high walled garden full of pots overflowing with multi-coloured plants. As we approached the front door, up some weathered stone steps, I was conscious of the intoxicating scent of flowers filling the air and also the lively bird song from birds I did not recognise. I turned to look back, thinking the garden had a very relaxed and natural feel and hoped this reflected the personality of the owner.

Jack walked straight into the house, so I followed him to be greeted by a small, very pretty woman with thick fair hair greying at the sides, cut in a gamin style. She was wearing smart black trousers with gold sandals and a chic white, thin cotton blouse. She had Jack's easy elegance and also his wide, ready smile. However, there was no sign of the dazzling blue eyes. Hers were dark brown, so I concluded that Jack had inherited his father's eyes at least.

I was made very welcome and immediately shown to my bedroom to freshen up whilst Jack's mother, Audrey, went downstairs to prepare some tea for us. I looked around and noticed the room had sunshine yellow striped wall paper with a green wall to wall carpet. The furniture was painted white and there was an attractive wicker chair by the window, that offered a view of the garden. The bedspread had a splodgy flower pattern on it and there were pretty cushions, including a large floor cushion in the corner. I remember it clearly as it was so beautifully done and very much a room of its era. In the bedside cabinet I saw two books. One was *The Hitchhikers Guide to the Galaxy* and the other was *Watership Down*. When I saw the former I immediately thought of Jake and suddenly had a longing to see him, which surprised me given where I was and with whom. I sat down on the wicker chair and collected my thoughts. Despite my wobble over Jake I realised that I was totally happy about everything and felt optimistic for the future.

The bathroom was next door. Instead of updating it, the bathroom had been restored to its former glory. There was a cast iron bath and large black radiator. The panelling was painted a rich plum colour and the elegant washstand was brilliant white. I noticed a lovely ornate mirror and an antique chair which was very comfortable when I sat on it. The room was finished off with a basket of grey and white towels and a ceramic bowl of fragrant rose pot pourri. I enjoyed splashing my face with cool water and scrubbing my hands with scented soap. I gave my hair a good brush to restore its lustre then skipped downstairs to seek out Jack and Audrey. The tea and cake were served in the conservatory at the back of the house. Audrey called the conservatory the sunroom and indeed the afternoon sun was streaming in, but the open doors kept it pleasantly cool. I felt very much at home as I sank into a plump sofa and helped myself to refreshments. We had chocolate sponge oozing with cream and cherries. It was made by a confectioner in a place called Barnard Castle, Audrey told us, and no it wasn't Black Forest Gateaux. The tea was delicious and made with real leaves, though Audrey admitted she sometimes used tea bags now they were fashionable, but not for special guests.

I listened with interest as Jack and Audrey chatted. It was lovely to hear their charming, soft Northumbrian accents. The stresses and strains of my punishing concert schedule began to melt away. After a while I could feel myself getting drowsy and despite my best efforts to stay awake I fell into a deep sleep. I awoke some time later to find I was covered with a light wool blanket. I could hear voices next door and turned to see Jack and his mother seated at a table by the window, both looking quite serious and obviously absorbed in conversation. After a while I rubbed the sleep from my eyes and jumped off the sofa with the blanket around my shoulders. I didn't feel any embarrassment as I entered the room next door.

"Hello!" said Jack, his face relaxing. He was looking amused.

"Hope you don't mind, Lara, we left you sleeping. You seemed so peaceful and we didn't want to disturb you," his mother added.

"Oh, that's fine. Thanks so much for the cover, it's lovely and cosy."

This was the start of what was to be a close relationship with Audrey. She was bright and fun to be with, but also had a kind and motherly manner. I discovered that she had been the head teacher of a local village primary school before retirement but now spent most of her time in the garden and being involved with the Women's' Institute. Later, she told me she would have liked a daughter, which sort of explained her warmth towards me. She had a way of making you feel cherished without being excessive.

The Durham Miners' Gala was the next day and Audrey gave us a lift into the city. I was captivated by what I saw. There were cobbled streets, boutiques and cafes, and although the city was tiny compared to London, it seemed to be buzzing with life. The sun was shining and there was an air of excitement. Jack grasped my hand and led me through the crush of people. I could hear a brass band playing somewhere and I felt my eyes fill up with tears. I recognised the music as *Gresford*, the miners' hymn, and had heard it many times when I was small and used to listen to my father playing it. Despite the dangers of the job he was truly happy then. He loved the camaraderie and really missed this when he was made redundant and became a long distance lorry driver.

We reached the racecourse and saw the brass band gathered. They started to move and march along, all the miners' unions represented with their different silk banners unfurling in the breeze. We joined the advancing crowd and followed the march. It finished at the university.

Jack told me, "There's a wonderful Art Deco chapel in the university. We must try to visit it sometime. I'd love to show you all the features, its splendid contours and discrete windows and especially the way the light plays on the plain, plastered walls during daytime." His way of speaking was rather formal, but even so his fervour for architecture and the way he described it enthralled me.

We listened to the passionate speeches and found them inspiring and at times moving. Some of the speakers looked familiar from television and I thought I recognised Shirley Williams and James Callaghan but I wasn't sure. Following political speeches and cheers from the crowd there was to be a service in the cathedral. As we walked away, Jack and I agreed it had all been very poignant and recognised the gala as a celebration of mining heritage and the trade union movement, but also a sad reminder of lives and jobs lost.

"Do you fancy a coffee?" Jack said. "Or something stronger?"

"No, coffee would be fine. Thanks," I replied. I felt in need of a caffeine boost and something sweet.

"I suggest we skip the service and go straight to the cafe before the crowds get there," he said.

Jack took my hand and we walked until I could see the magnificent Norman cathedral standing dominant high above the river bank and woodland. Jack explained it was built on a sort of peninsula created by a loop in the River Wear. From the outside it looked almost like three cathedrals, it was so complex, and to my surprise he drew me inside. I hadn't realised the cafe was within the cathedral. The staff were very welcoming and understood perfectly when Jack said we needed coffee. We walked past some amazing tombs and I had to stop to admire them. One was dedicated to St Cuthbert and another to the Venerable Bede. I had heard of them both but knew nothing of their history, so I was pleased when Jack gave me a brief lecture about them. I don't remember much of it now except that St Bede was a great Anglo Saxon scholar who wrote and translated about four hundred books on practically every area of knowledge, and St Cuthbert, also Anglo Saxon, was responsible for the spread of Christianity in the North of England.

I was awestruck by the magnificence of the building. I remember there were huge pillars with ornate zigzag and diamond carvings and a beautiful rose window in one of the chapels. Some of the windows were modern and nowadays there is a Millennium window, which I love. It depicts scenes from St Cuthbert's life and many of the trades and industries associated with County Durham, like the coal mines. I spent a few minutes examining the altar, which was covered in medieval carvings, and was mesmerised by a gorgeous medieval clock. We wandered through the cloisters and admired the wonderful vaulting. The cafe was called the Undercroft and was below the south side of the cloisters. I remember it all so well, having now visited this fine cathedral with my husband and family many times. I even played my cello there once, as a member of a string quartet, to raise money for the Children in Need appeal.

As its name suggests, the cafe was in the undercroft and in spite of its location there seemed to be a warm atmosphere and a soft hum of conversation. No doubt some people had taken refuge, like us, from the noise of the gala crowds.

Once seated with coffee and cake, Jack began to talk about the modern mining industry in the Durham area. He spoke with intensity and knowledge.

"The Durham coalfields covered north east and central Durham and were nationalised in 1947."

"When did the first mines open?" I asked. I was keen to know more as my father had never spoken about the history of his job.

"Well, mining here dates back to the thirteenth century when there was widespread excavation and it peaked in about 1913. In 1923 there were one hundred and seventy thousand miners, would you believe? Unfortunately the mines declined after the Second World War and many pits closed in the 1950s and 1960s."

"It's hard to see where the mines have been, isn't it?" I commented.

"Yes, because many pit heaps have been reclaimed into the natural landscape, which is really good. Sadly it wasn't so good for the miners, as you know, and the closures had shattering consequences for many families."

We were both quiet for a while as we reflected on this. Little did we know that there would be major industrial action ten years later in 1984, and this would result in defeat and a significantly weakened Trade Union movement. In several pits the wives distributed carnations at the gates on the day the miners went back, and these were known as the hero flowers. Some miners marched with brass bands and I think that must have been an emotional sight. I remember watching it on the television news.

"Are you sorry you didn't become a miner?" I asked Jack.

He smiled and squeezed my shoulder gently but didn't reply.

We caught a bus back to Jack's village and arrived in time for our evening meal. Audrey was very chatty and opened a bottle of wine. The conversation was soon flowing.

"So, tell me all about it," Audrey said eagerly. I was surprised she was so keen to discuss it as I assumed it would bring to mind her husband's death. Then I remembered Jack saying she seemed to be coping well before he took off for the continent. I guessed she must be a very stable person with strong faith. I discovered later that, although they were close, she and her husband lived quite independent lives and her faith was in her own self-belief.

The next day, Jack asked if I would mind if he went to visit friends in Durham and suggested that I spend some time with Audrey.

"The garden's gorgeous at this time, and I'm sure she'd love to show you round."

"Yes, I'd love that too. I know next to nothing about gardens but I really like flowers," I said, pleased at the opportunity to be with his mother, whose cordial manner had made me feel really welcome.

I was struck by the complete peacefulness of the garden after the noise and bustle of London. Immediately outside the back door there was a courtyard surrounded by a red brick wall. Audrey explained that they called it the walled garden.

"It's pretentious, I know," she said, "but it describes it perfectly."

Within the walls I could smell the scent from a deep red climbing rose which Audrey called "the scarlet woman". There was a raised bed made from old railway sleepers with a fountain in the centre. The sound of the water splashing and the bird song was very relaxing. Audrey pointed out different birds and told me their names. There were blackbirds, which I recognised, and goldfinches, siskins and longtailed tits all eating at the feeders. They looked rather exotic to me, but apparently they were quite common garden birds.

"My husband, John, gave me the fountain as a birthday present. It's lovely isn't it?" Audrey said.

"Yes, it's really beautiful and I adore the sound of water. It's so tranquil," I replied.

"When I retired, I had more time for gardening, and when John died I found it very therapeutic," she said, almost without emotion, yet with that characteristic familial bowing of the head which I had observed in Jack.

Audrey led me down some steps into a colourful terraced area which she explained had been created on the site of an old kitchen garden.

"Jack wanted us to renovate the kitchen garden. You know what he's like with his cooking, but we wanted something different with cascades of flowers and alpines. We were given quite a few artefacts by good friends which we were able to recycle." She pointed out some small stone figures, flagstones, and ancient pots. "We also used all sorts of things which we collected from holidays, like these."

She drew my attention to a lithe Art Deco woman fashioned in lead, which was Jack's favourite, and had been brought back from the Algarve. There was also her favourite, a delightful tiny limestone seahorse from Italy.

I was fascinated by her story of how the garden had been created. It was obviously a labour of love and partnership. I could see how it would bring joy but also be a sorrowful reminder of John's passing.

Eventually Audrey led me back up to the house and we sat in quietness on an old cedar bench, made comfortable with green check cushions.

"Tell you what. Shall I bring out some lunch and we can just relax and chat until Jack comes back?" she said.

"That would be brilliant," I said enthusiastically. "Thank you. Shall I come inside and help?"

"Oh no, love, you stay here and enjoy the garden. I know you must need a break. Being a concert musician is hard work, I'm sure. From what Jack tells me you live, eat and breathe cello!"

"Well I do take time off, particularly where food is concerned." I laughed, wondering what else Jack had said about me.

"Good, that's settled. Back in a jiffy." Audrey disappeared indoors.

It was about twenty minutes later that she returned, carrying a tray laden with food and a bottle of wine with glasses. She laid it all on a table by the bench and immediately poured us a drink. It was a sparkling wine called Asti Spumante which I'd never tried before. Then she sat down, kicked off her sandals and sighed with contentment.

"It's so good to have you here. I miss young company. We're all old fogies in the W.I. And I don't see much of Jack or his brother."

"I didn't know Jack had a brother," I said, bewildered.

"Oh, sorry, I thought he would have mentioned Rob. He's Jack's twin. Not that you would guess. They look so different and are unlike in so many ways. But you'll find out more about that when you meet Rob," she said with a twinkle in her eye.

I could sense myself being drawn into the family circle and I was slightly unnerved at this, not knowing whether I was ready for it. Fortunately, Audrey indicated the food and invited me to eat.

"I forgot to check if you're vegetarian, but there should be enough choice if you are," she said.

"Well, no not really, but Jack introduced me to the joys of pasta with veggie sauce and I must admit I was very impressed."

"I'm sure you were. Jack's a wonderful cook and uses such interesting ingredients. I haven't heard of most of them!"

"Same here," I agreed, though I was surprised at her modesty when I surveyed the delicious food she had laid out. There were green and black olives, devilled eggs, celery stuffed with tuna, tiny salmon and cucumber sandwiches, crisps, cheese and crackers and a big bowl of strawberries. I helped myself, trying not to let my mouth water.

Jack's mother ate very little but I couldn't help noticing that the bottle of wine soon disappeared and she produced another one, filling up our glasses.

The more Audrey drank the more chatty she became. At first she was very animated when telling me stories of her life in teaching, some of them quite humorous. I could see where Jack got his sense of fun and hoped his *joie de vivre* would return soon. Audrey asked me a lot of questions about my family and my home and I found myself opening up in a way I never had before.

Audrey paused for a while and her face became more serious. Her only wrinkle was a small furrow over her right brow and I recalled that Jack had a similar one

"Come. I want to show you something," she said standing up and grasping my hand. She was slightly unsteady with the wine but succeeded in leading me down the steps and round the corner.

There I was surprised to see a large pond surrounded by huge plants and grasses.

"Look!" she said excitedly.

I was mesmerised by the sight of some beautiful long winged insects dancing over the water.

"What are they?" I asked.

"The bigger ones are dragonflies and the smaller slender ones are damselflies," she replied. "We're very lucky to have them. You're more likely to see them by rivers and streams on warm days."

"They're gorgeous. Their wings are like gossamer and such wonderful translucent blues and greens. They're almost like fairies," I said.

"You have such a lovely imagination. I can see why Jack is so fond of you," she replied. "Why don't we sit awhile?" She led me to a curved stone bench covered by a soft blue and white throw folded into a cushion.

"I often sit here to enjoy the quietness," Audrey said.

For a while we didn't speak, then suddenly she looked directly at me and smiled.

"You know Jack's father died in a car crash?" she said. Then without waiting for an answer she continued, "Well, there's something I want to share with you. I've discussed it with Jack and he would like you to know."

I was now feeling rather uncomfortable and was afraid the exquisiteness of the past few minutes was about to be erased. It brought to mind the moment when my mother told me she had been diagnosed with multiple sclerosis. We were sitting in our little back garden like this enjoying a pot of tea and scones, then in an instant my world turned upside down.

I hesitated then gave Audrey a nod of compliance.

"Jack's father was very depressed about his work when he died, and we believe he crashed the car with the intention of taking his own life." Audrey spoke quietly and with deliberation.

She rose and touched me gently on the shoulder.

"You stay here in the sunshine. I'll make us some coffee indoors," she said, as if nothing had happened.

I felt numb and focussed hard on a damselfly which had landed on a large, glossy leaf on the pond.

I was conscious of the intoxicating, almost overpowering perfume from the tall pink lilies in the pot by the bench. I felt close to fainting.

My mind was filled with sadness for Jack and his mother but also for myself at the memory of my own mother's early death. At the same time I was humming snatches from Elgar's cello concerto under my breath. Without warning there was a flash of blue and the delicate insect was caught by a bird. The whole experience seemed to encapsulate my life both present and future.

When Jack and I returned home I didn't see him for about a week. I was glad as I needed time to think. Then he phoned to ask if I wanted to meet at his studio for the unveiling of the portrait. I couldn't wait but felt nervous at the same time, unsure how I would react if I didn't like it. I needn't have worried, for the portrait was a thing of beauty and flattered me greatly. I gasped with appreciation. Still, there was a strangeness about it and as I moved away to see it better I realised that in the picture my face was more like that of a handsome boy than a young woman. I wondered if this was how people saw me. When I caught glimpses of myself in a mirror I was always surprised at how feminine I looked in spite of my great height.

"What do you think of it?" Jack said.

"It's wonderful. You've really caught my expression and I love the cello. It looks so real. To be honest, though, I think you've done your best to beautify me, and for that I'm grateful!" I replied with a laugh.

"Good. I'm glad it meets with your approval. Now, I'll let you have it on one condition."

"Yes, and what might that be?" I said.

Jack's proposal didn't take long. I remember he came across and took hold of my hands. I felt my heart jump, dreading what might come next. To be honest I'm not exactly sure what he said but it was something like this: "I'd like you to hang the portrait on a wall in our house."

I'm sure I must have looked puzzled as Jack then added, "What I mean is, will you marry me?"

For a minute I said nothing but held fast to his hands and examined his face. His eyes were deepest blue and his expression was alert but relaxed. How could I resist? I knew I had passed the potential partner test with his mother and I knew he would make me happy. I did not feel for Jack the extreme passion I felt for Jake but that was just a memory to store and retrieve from time to time.

"Sorry, I can see my proposal has taken you by surprise. Do take a few days to think about it..."

I laughed. "I don't need to Jack. Yes, I will marry you, otherwise I'll never get my picture!"

Jack joined in my laughter and we hugged each other.

"Lara, bonny lass, I'm so pleased. I'll take care of you and do everything I can to make you happy."

Then he said something which I didn't really understand.

"I'm sure I can live a normal life with you at my side."

I assumed he thought I could help ease the pain of the loss of his father and I hoped I could, for Jack was such a loving man and I was already beginning to love him.

CHAPTER EIGHT

JAKE

I couldn't wait to surprise Lara and felt elated as I approached her front door. When she opened it her cheeks blushed and her mouth widened in a smile.

"Jake!" she exclaimed, clearly astonished at the sight of me. "Please come in... it's lovely to see you. I thought you'd disappeared forever."

I followed her into the tiny front parlour with its attractive bay window. It was just as I remembered, rather cluttered with books and flowers, but comfortable nevertheless.

"Sorry to call without warning but I'm only in London for a short visit and I didn't want to miss seeing you. It's been a long time and I know it's your birthday sometime around now," I said.

"Yes, it is," she replied. "How good of you to remember. It must be a year ago that I last saw you at my birthday party. Anyhow, now you're here you must sit down and tell me everything."

She sat beside me on the somewhat lumpy sofa then immediately jumped up again. She seemed a little on edge.

"Sorry, I should have offered you a drink," she said. I opened the bag I'd brought with me to reveal a bottle of Dom Perignon.

"Will this do?" I asked.

"It certainly will," she replied. "I suppose it is a cause for celebration, your appearing so unexpectedly. I'll fetch some glasses."

"I'll come with you and uncork the champers. It's liable to go all over the place," I said.

We returned to the sofa with drinks and crisps. Lara and I found ourselves examining each other, no doubt observing any changes in appearance or demeanour. We caught ourselves doing this and both laughed out loud.

"You're looking into my soul again," she said with a smile.

"You look wonderful, Lara. You're obviously happy with life."

"Yes, I'm feeling pretty good right now. How about you? You look really fit and tanned. Have you been abroad again?" she asked.

"Yes... I've been working in Chile for a while."

We both took a drink in non-matching glasses and Lara ate a few crisps. Then she looked at me cautiously and said, "I have some news. Jack Greenhill and I are to be married in a few weeks. You remember Jack, don't you?" She paused, waiting for my reaction.

"That's marvellous, Lara. I didn't realise you and Jack were so close. Well, actually, I never really met him, did I, so I guess I wouldn't have known. It's a bit of a surprise but I really am pleased for you. Let's have another glass to toast your forthcoming wedding."

I decided not to share my own news.

We finished off the bottle and Lara was intoxicated and clearly elated. I knew what would happen next and made no attempt to control the situation. My passion for Lara was pure and not bound by morality or circumstances. There was the realisation for both of us that this would be the last time we would experience such intimacy.

Afterwards, Lara led me to the music room and beckoned me to sit on one of the battered stools whilst she played a rather melancholy cello piece. I could see she was crying. We were startled out of the reverie by a ring at the doorbell. Lara wiped her eyes with the hem of her top and stood up.

"I'll be back in a minute. It's probably Felice, my housemate, she's always forgetting her keys."

I sat and waited and was curious when I heard the sound of a male voice. There were two lots of footsteps walking down the corridor towards the music room and then the door was pushed open to reveal Lara with a pleasant looking man. Lara seemed slightly nervous but on the whole she hid her feelings well. I stood up and smiled.

"Jacob, this is my fiancée Jack. I was just explaining you're on a brief visit to London and had called in to see me."

"Hello, Jack. It's good to meet you. Lara was telling me all about you. Wonderful news that you're getting married. She's a gorgeous girl. You beat me to it!" I said. This was possibly a little careless as both Jack and Lara looked uncomfortable. I took this as my cue to depart.

"Look, I need to make tracks now. It's been brilliant to catch up Lara, and I'm really glad to have met you, Jack. I hope all goes well with the wedding plans... let me know," I said. "It would be nice to keep in touch."

As they accompanied me to the door, Jack said, "When do you leave London, Jacob?" I liked his mellow North East accent and he seemed a decent sort of person who would make a good friend and a good husband for Lara.

"I'll be leaving the day after tomorrow. I've got a couple more friends to catch up with," I replied. "Also my Papa lives in London so I'll be calling on him too."

"Are you staying close by?"

"Yes, quite near. It's the Langham," I said. I noticed a bunch of yellow roses on the hall table. I guessed they must be Lara's favourite flowers.

"Goodbye Jake," Lara said, touching my hand. She looked down and was clearly still ill at ease.

"Bye, both of you," I replied. "Take care and be happy."

I walked away, then turned and raised my hand in a farewell gesture.

"Cheerio Jacob. Enjoy the rest of your stay," Jack shouted. They both disappeared indoors.

The next day is one I shall never forget. It was about six p.m. and I was watching the evening news in my hotel room. There was a knock at the door and when I opened it I was surprised to see Jack standing there. For the first time I was aware of his physical presence, which was unusual for me as I normally only take notice of how women look. Women and the universe are my two obsessions.

Jack was smaller than me and much stockier. He was also much more stylish in his pure white shirt, indigo sweater and good jeans. I always looked a bit unkempt I think with my faded old clothes and unruly black curly hair.

"Oh, hello, Jack," I said. "This is an unexpected pleasure."

Without warning Jack threw a left hook and punched me on the nose. I fell backwards against the wall with the force of it. Before he could hit me again I put up my fists to protect my face and was conscious of blood dripping down my cheek. Jack hesitated and I pushed him away

"What the hell are you playing at?" I said.

He brushed back his thick hair with his hand then steadied himself against the door. He bowed his head and I sensed that the fight, such as it was, had come to an end.

Jack raised his head and looked directly at me. I remember being startled by the colour of his eyes, which brought to mind an inky night sky. I now understood what Lara meant when she accused me of looking into her soul. I felt Jack could see into mine.

"Jacob man, I'm sorry," he faltered. "The way you and Lara were together, the way she played for you... I felt as if I was losing her. I was so angry but I came round to talk, not to thump you."

I wanted to laugh as the situation was so ridiculous, but the blood was making its way slowly down to my neck and I could feel a bump appearing under my eye. This distracted me from Jack's apology and my main concern was to clean myself up.

"Here, take this," Jack said, offering me a pristine white handkerchief.

"Thanks," I replied, glad of the opportunity to get my own back by ruining Jack's hanky.

I thought for a second then asked Jack if he would like to come in and talk.

"Yes," he said. "Perhaps that'll give us a chance to clear the air. I promise I'll behave."

He followed me in and we sat on hotel chairs opposite each other.

"What about a drink?" I said. "I've brought a decent scotch with me and I hate drinking alone."

"Fine... I prefer ale but I guess a scotch would calm me down."

Drinks in hand, we eyed each other for a minute like two caged animals unsure what to do next.

"So, do you want to talk?" I invited. "Before we do, I'd like to share something with you."

Jack looked apprehensive until I said, "I'm getting married, too, in a few weeks, to Helen, my fiancée. Lara was so full of her own wedding plans that I didn't have the opportunity to tell her, so you will mention it, won't you?"

That news immediately improved the atmosphere and after a few whiskies we were chatting like old friends. He really was very good company and a fount of knowledge.

When Jack came to leave I felt reluctant to see him go. I could sense why Lara wanted to marry him. He was very easy to be with. We shook hands and I observed that Jack's fingers were long and slender and his hands were almost feminine in shape. The hands of an artist. His grip was very strong and there was a warmth about his manner.

"Well, all the best for your wedding," he said.

"Likewise. Hope we can keep in touch now we're friends," I said, no doubt with a chuckle. "Oh, and do please call me Jake. All my friends do."

I had no idea that it was the last time I would see Jack, and it would be many years before I would see Lara again.

CHAPTER NINE

NAZ

Josh and I were born on the 13th January 1976. There the similarity ended. When our father, Jack, died, the British Consulate informed the UK police and they sent someone to break the news to Lara, my mother. She took them into the front sitting room and when they asked if she wanted me to be there she·said no and closed the door. A few minutes later I heard her sobbing and then she went quiet. When he heard, Josh went to the pub and got paralytic whilst I took to my bed and cried for hours. I must have fallen asleep at some point because I was awakened by the sound of hushed voices by the bedroom door. I heard Josh say, "Leave him Mum. You know what he's like. He'll need time to himself to recover his equilibrium." They closed the door gently. That was Josh, always right, always in control. Don't get me wrong, I loved him dearly, but I thought twins should be more compatible. I thought I resembled my father more, with his mercurial temperament, and Josh was more stable and resilient like my mother. How we were the same, was in our artistry. Mum had music, dad had drawing and painting, I had landscape gardening and Josh had architecture. So much creative genius under one roof was at times exhilirating and at times daunting. Sometimes I longed to live in an ordinary home with pop music on the radio, my mum hoovering and my dad cleaning the car.

I loved my job, apart from being accountable to Josh. I was also pretty good at it, too, judging by the feedback.

My father died in 2002 when I was twenty-six years old. My mother said he became a bit depressed because he felt he'd run out of inspiration, so they agreed he would take a trip to Italy, one of his favourite places, to regenerate his batteries. He insisted on going by motorbike of course. I remember he packed his metal panniers with painting gear and a few clothes. "I won't be away long," he said.

There were one or two postcards from Umbria and a couple of phone calls. Then, suddenly, all communication stopped for about a week. As I said, the news of my father's disappearance came via the police. His motorbike had been found in the mud on the bank of a fast flowing river at the bottom of a gorge, and some of his belongings were scattered around on the bank, including a letter from my mother, which identified him. It was assumed, naturally, that my father had drowned, although no body could be found when the river was dredged. My mother was distraught. The Italian police said there had been many accidents at this point in the road, as there was a very steep bend and people often travelled too fast in poor weather conditions. There had been two other fatalities that year and the bodies were only discovered months later, as the rapids carried them much further down river. My mother never really recovered because she could not bury her dead husband, so there was always a lack of closure.

She said, "I didn't say goodbye, at least not a last goodbye. I would have hugged him. I didn't get to do anything."

This was followed by a sort of denial when she seemed unable to believe Jack was dead.

She kept saying, "But he's only missing. He may not be dead."

For weeks her sleep was disrupted and she could not eat. I would hear her playing plaintive cello pieces at unusual hours of the day and night. Her favourites were *Sakura, Sakura* (an easy arrangement of a Japanese folk song) and Guillio Caccini's *Ave Maria*. Gradually, she came to terms with her bereavement, but even years later, birthdays and anniversaries triggered her grief once more. She said she sometimes felt frightened and lonely in spite of all her friends and family, as Jack had been her rock.

My own distress was driven by the loss of a father whom I worshipped because he seemed to understand me and my idiosyncracies. Josh, on the other hand, experienced a more manageable grief, which he kept in check by focusing on his social networks and career ambitions.

My mother was determined to mark my father's death in some way, so she decided several months later to invite all our family and friends to a memorial service. It was held at a little church hall in the village where dad's mother, Audrey, still lived. Nana was very old but still quite agile and quick witted. We used to go up a lot to visit her and had some lovely times walking in the Durham dales and exploring neighbouring villages. We always ate well, as Dad was the chef and

Nana provided the wine she was very fond of. The conversation flowed and we laughed a lot.

On the day of the memorial service, the hall was packed, with some people having to stand at the back. Mum bravely played a beautiful, haunting cello version of *God only knows* by the Beach Boys and I read a poem, whilst Josh spoke at length about our father. The poem was one I'd found amongst my father's things after his death and I assumed it had some significance for him. It was called *The Road Not Taken* by Robert Frost, of whom I'd never heard. I copied it out before reading it aloud and it has stayed with me.

"Two roads diverged in a yellow wood
And sorry I could not travel both
And be one traveller, long I stood
And looked down as far as I could
To where it bent in the undergrowth.

Then took the other, as just as fair
And having perhaps the better claim
Because it was grassy and wanted wear
Though as for that the passing there
Had worn them really about the same.

And both that morning equally lay
In leaves no step had trodden black
Oh, I kept the first for another day!
Yet knowing how way may lead on to way
I doubted if I should ever come back.

I shall be telling this with a sigh
Somewhere ages and ages hence:
Two roads diverged in a wood, and I -
I took the one less travelled by.
And that made all the difference."

I thought the poem rather appealing in a naïve sort of way. Apparently it was intended as a gentle mocking of indecision, as observed in a friend with whom the poet walked. When I introduced it I was conscious that my voice sounded strange and trembly. I breathed deeply and settled my nerves so that I was in control and able to speak the words with quiet confidence. I remember starting to enjoy the experience and wished my father had been there to hear me.

Josh's eulogy for my father was a far more humorous and down to earth affair. He illustrated his tribute with well-chosen stories which, although amusing, managed to convey a sense of my father's kindness, energy, optimism and imagination. Josh also referred to my father's capacity for giving advice and information, even if not required, and his fondness for dominating situations and sharing his opinions on all subjects. Josh was very adept at mimicking my father's Northumbrian accent.

There were nods of agreement and ripples of quiet laughter but the respect for my father was undeniable. Josh gave a remarkable account of what it was like to be Jack's son and a twin. The only sign of nerves was a slightly shaky hand when he flicked over his notes, and I don't think anyone else would have noticed.

Mum had displayed a lot of my father's work around the hall and also posters by an artist called Cassandre, who was Dad's hero when he was a student. I discovered by accident when looking through my father's papers that Cassandre died on June 17th, the same date that my father is believed to have died, but many years previously, in 1968. I thought this an eerie coincidence and was shocked to find that Cassandre committed suicide. It was a few years later that mum told me and Josh that Nana's husband also committed suicide. Josh showed no evidence of being upset by this and just said, "It happens," shrugging his shoulders. I was concerned there might be a predisposition in our family to take our own lives. I did a lot of research on the subject but didn't reach any conclusions and eventually let go of the thought. The only bit I really remember is that there are studies suggesting that creative people are more likely to suffer from mood disorders. There certainly seemed to be a long list of artists who did take their own lives and there was even a degree of creativity in the methods chosen.

Anyway, one interesting occurrence at the memorial service was the appearance of my maternal grandfather, Ernest Ackroyd. We had met him only a couple of times, because following his wife's death from Multiple Sclerosis he went abroad to Japan and did not return. This was an unusual move for an ex-miner from West Yorkshire, but my mother said he read widely and was fascinated by the history and culture of the East. She thought he was seeking solace and was not surprised when he met and married a Japanese woman twenty years his junior. Her name was Karin, and when we were introduced to her we agreed with what he had written in a letter: that she was an undemanding and compassionate woman. She had a stillness about her which was very engaging. She was right for him and he settled happily in Japan, recovering from the years of sorrow he had suffered watching my grandmother deteriorate and finally die.

I recognised my grandfather immediately as he was so like my mother, tall and striking in appearance. He had a good head of hair, now sandy in colour, and a neat greying moustache. Close up his eyes were a greeny hazel and his face bore that lopsided appearance which was a family trait.

When he entered the village hall I noticed he was carrying his trumpet and indeed he played his own arrangement of a piece of music which he called *Kaki*. It sounded like *Summertime* from Porgy and Bess to me, so I was not surprised when he said later that Kaki meant summertime in Japanese. It was a joyful sound and contrasted well with my mother's cello piece. Grandfather's wife, Karin, still looked very youthful with her delicate features and porcelain skin. Her black hair was thick and glossy and done in rather an old fashioned way. She was very well groomed, as befitted a professional woman, and had a gracious smile which she seemed to ration and only bestowed when she felt it was totally appropriate. We chatted after the service and I was surprised when they invited me and Josh to fly out and stay with them. They were keen to show us the cherry blossom trees. Josh was really taken with Karin and said we would be delighted to join them for a short holiday the following March. I didn't really have a say but thought on the whole it might be interesting and I might get some inspiration for my landscape work.

Thus we travelled to Tokyo the following year at the end of March, just in time for the start of the cherry blossom festival. My grandfather and Karin lived in a four storey house in a densely populated area. The house had a stunning huge triangular window positioned above the double height living room, which was on the second floor, and the window was set at an angle to bring light across the space and through the kitchen and bedroom just behind. I was fascinated by it and wondered if it was an idea I could use to effect in my landscaping designs. My grandfather and Karin took us to stay for a few days in a traditional inn, or ryokan, where we relaxed unwinding in hot springs and dining on kaiseki Japanese cuisine. The food was a work of art and delicious. There were many courses including tiny delicate appetisers, slices of raw fish, soup, Japanese hotpot, rice and desserts. Karin told us all the food was seasonal and very fresh and the chefs prided themselves on using flowers and leaves to garnish the dishes. They certainly looked delightful. Grandfather and Karin thought we would enjoy the sights more if we had recovered from our work exhaustion, and they were right.

When we went out the streets were clogged with revellers and the parks full of families having picnics under the falling petals of the blossom trees. In the evening there were lanterns lighting the trees and food and sake was available. People sang songs to celebrate the coming of the spring. It was enchanting. Karin told us that the trees were loved for their obvious beauty but also, as the blossom was short-lived, they were regarded as something transient and melancholy. The songs announced a graceful resignation to the cherry trees' passing. Strangely I found this notion helpful in coming to terms with my father's death.

Josh was bewitched by everything Japanese. Before our departure at the end of April, Karin arranged a little social event. She invited a few friends, many of them younger people around our age, and most of them were fashionably late. I suppose it was inevitable that Josh would fall in love with one of the guests. I watched it happen and was moved by the almost immediate attraction between him and Hana. It was a quiet and gentle courtship, completely out of character for Josh. They seemed to be captivated by each other and he said later that he knew this was what he had been waiting for.

Josh and Hana married that summer and lived in Josh's house in inner London. It was a tall, Georgian terrace house built in 1760 and had belonged to a coal merchant. Sadly, it had lost much of its charm and Josh, who bought it for a song, couldn't wait to give it the kiss of life. It became his hobby and Hana was just as enthusiastic. They had fun tracking down old fireplaces, ceiling mouldings, firegrates, and even furniture which would help restore their home to its former glory. As for me, I much preferred the simplicity of contemporary architecture, though I admired their achievement and the house looked wonderful when they had completed it.

It was after our visit to Japan, having returned home without a sweetheart, that I overheard my mother in the studio saying bizarre things to a photograph of someone called Jake. I was determined to find out the truth. First of all I decided to talk to Josh about it. I arranged to see him in the pub on the pretext of telling him the news about my competition win.

"Hey, what a star you are. Well done, old chap. So when do you start the contract?" he said, genuinely pleased for me. That was typical of Josh, so open and generous of spirit.

"I'm not too sure. But I'll need to talk to you about how it's going to work with the business," I replied.

"Fine. We can do that as soon as you have more info. Brilliant!"

We sat in silence, both lost in thought, and drank some more beer.

"I need to talk to you about something else, Josh," I said tentatively.

"Don't tell me you're getting married, too," he said with a smile. "Sorry, only joking. Go on then, spill the beans."

He obviously didn't think me capable of falling in love but I decided not to pursue this, as I knew from past experience it would only lead to conflict. I had to share the burden of what I had heard, so I plunged in and recounted the incident in the studio exactly as it had occurred.

"She said what?" said Josh in disbelief. "Tell me again."

"She was in the studio and was holding a photograph, presumably taken from the portmanteau. She gazed at it and said, 'Jake, I love you still'. Then moments later, 'You are the father of my three children'."

"But that doesn't make any sense, Naz. Are you sure she didn't say 'Jack'?"

I made a non-committal gesture and sat in silence awaiting further reassurance from Josh.

Surprisingly it wasn't forthcoming. Instead he said, "So what do you intend to do about it?"

"I'm not sure whether to do anything. I could be completely wrong...What do you think?"

"I don't really know. I suppose you could try to get a look at the photograph and then decide." I noticed he didn't include himself in this venture, which led me to believe that he thought the whole matter was nonsense. This made me feel a bit easier in my mind.

"Yes, I wondered about doing that myself, but I'd feel a bit guilty sneaking about in the studio. That's if Mum's left the photograph there. I'm assuming she put it back in the portmanteau."

"Do you fancy another pint?" Josh said, getting back to normality.

"Yes, my turn I think." I was glad of the opportunity to stretch my legs and ponder on my conversation with Josh. His reaction had been more subdued than I expected and when I returned with the drinks he seemed very pensive. When I looked at him I saw myself in his face for the first time. I was accustomed to seeing the same bushy red brown hair, pale blue eyes, long thin face and prominent nose. He even had the same little furrow across one brow. But more startling was I could sense that our expressions at that moment were identical. It was an alarming experience. I wasn't sure I liked the idea that we were the same after all. Even more extraordinary was the fact that I could tell Josh recognised himself in me for the first time also and this seemed to confound him.

"OK?" I said.

"Yeah... sure," he replied. "Cheers!"

Afterwards, we went our separate ways and I was left to figure out on my own whether to forget my mother's curious conversation with a photograph or take action that might unleash demons.

Somehow the issue would not go away, but I decided to leave the problem on one side for a while and concentrate on my new contract. For once I made the right decision, because as well as the distraction of a stimulating new job, I also fell in love and the photograph incident diminished in importance, so much so that eventually I never gave it another thought.

CHAPTER TEN

JOSH

When Naz told me in the pub about the incident involving my mother and the photograph, I was shocked but hardly surprised. Since being a teenager I had sensed that there was some mystery in the family, and I always thought my father and mother behaved more like affectionate siblings than husband and wife. Although I'd felt obliged to point out to Naz the ridiculousness of the situation, I could not bring myself to reassure him as I think he expected me to. Whilst he was able to put the issue on one side to concentrate on the new contract he'd won, I was determined to get to the bottom of the story. Everyone assumed I was the calm, stable one who took everything in my stride, but I wasn't so unlike Naz. After all, we were twins. I had always needed to feel secure and in control. If I wasn't, my creativity and ambition tended to dip. I had to learn the truth about our mother's secret, if there was one. I wasn't sure whether or not to consult Hana, my wife, and I needed to think about that before acting. We shared everything and I didn't want to deceive her in any way, and yet I wasn't sure if she would understand my dilemma. She might think this affair was a small thing and that Naz and I were worrying about nothing. But, like Naz, I had a strong emotional connection with my father and the idea that my mother may have betrayed him made me incredibly angry. The notion that my true father might be someone different tied a knot in my stomach.

A couple of weeks later I had a phone call from Naz. He sounded very excited. "Hi Josh. Just wanted to let you know Greenglobe have got a contract for me. It's with a guy called Dr Newman who's the director of a new observatory near Cambridge. He's got a load of funding for a project to develop the observatory and re-design the grounds to make it all more appealing to visitors. But the best news is that, as well as my landscaping work, he also wants to expand the observatory itself and needs an imaginative architect to take this on. Apparently he knew we were brothers and he's familiar with our work, so he suggested you might be interested in tendering. What do you think?"

I was quite taken aback by this. It was very unexpected and I wasn't sure if I was interested. I was keen for Naz to go it alone for once and had no desire to butt in.

"Hm. I'm not really sure Naz. It's your project and I have a lot of work on already."

"Oh... are you sure? It would have been great having you on board and I'd still be doing my own thing, you know. Please consider it. I'm due to meet Dr Newman next week. I could let you know what he's like..."

"Actually, I've never come across him before. Have you, Naz?"

"Only through the newspaper. He was knighted for services to astronomy last year. I can't remember exactly what he's famous for, but I know he did a lot of original work on galaxies, something to do with their formation and evolution. I think he had a partnership going with some Japanese astro physicists..... he doesn't seem to use his title."

"I didn't realise he was an astronomer. I thought he was probably a civil servant of some description. That could be quite an interesting project. Maybe I will consider applying."

"Great! Shall I let him know, Josh?"

"Yeah, if you wish. Thanks. Look, I have to go. I have a client to see, so talk to you later."

"OK. See you later Josh. Bye."

I put down the phone and spent a minute or two reflecting on my conversation with Naz. The idea of working with an astronomer appealed to me. Designing part of a new observatory was certainly different and I knew it would be a stimulating project.

A week later Naz had the meeting with Dr Newman and his team. He came back with glowing reports.

"The observatory is amazing and it's surrounded by fields and woodland which they want me to incorporate into my landscaping."

"So did you tell him I'd like to tender for the architectural work?" I said.

"Of course, and Dr Newman said he'll send you a briefing of his requirements and then you can put forward some ideas."

"Great! Thanks a lot Naz. I owe you one. Do you fancy running through your landscaping ideas with me so that I can bear them in mind?"

"Sure."

Naz looked as pleased as punch. He was obviously thrilled that he'd done something to help me for a change. He admitted he'd been greatly influenced by a garden he had visited a couple of years ago, whilst on holiday in Scotland.

"We were lucky. The garden only opens once a year and we happened to be in the area, so we took the opportunity. I'd heard it was one of the best contemporary gardens in the country, designed by an American landscape architect, Charles Jencks, in collaboration with his wife and some other experts, scientists and academics. It was called 'The Garden of Cosmic Speculation'.

Naz was very animated as he described what sounded like a unique and beautiful garden full of vast sculpted earthworks, lakes, pathways and amazing engineered structures. It covered thirty acres and comprised forty major areas, each one different. They had names like the black hole terrace, the DNA garden, and the cascading universe. Naz's arms were all over the place as he tried to demonstrate the huge spirals and twisted, undulating landforms within the garden. He was such a child, but he had that special touch of genius too.

"When you're there you feel as if you're looking at the universe in miniature. It's almost like being *Alice in Wonderland*. The designers have somehow succeeded in combining the beauty of nature with modern science and mathematics. I remember the garden information said something like the designers were inspired by cosmology and the dynamic interactions between the unfolding universe, an evolving science and a questioning design!" He laughed.

"I wasn't really sure what that meant but it certainly gave me a few ideas about the potential for designing on a cosmic scale and using modern materials and space age concepts. The other really good thing was the garden taught me about the importance of humour in design if it's to appeal to the average person in the street."

Naz stressed that his own design was very different and when he showed me the drafts on computer, I could see what he meant. I was impressed at how he had exploited the natural advantages of the landscape around the observatory and had created an alien but alluring world which would appeal to children and adults alike. There were lots of online applications enabling visitors to explore many fascinating aspects of astronomy. You could look at a sky map, new planet discoveries, galaxies, black holes and even an imaginary human colony on Mars. There were interactive games, educational cartoons, quizzes and puzzles, which all seemed a lot of fun. It was almost like an adventure playground created by the mind of a science fiction writer. Naz had cleverly harmonised this with a few acres of gardens and woodland. He had made lavish use of gigantic plants like tree ferns, palms, monkey puzzle trees and quite a few which I didn't recognise. These were planted close together so that you caught occasional glimpses of the sky. The most striking feature was a rooftop garden reached by a series of ramps. There was a dark pool on the roof which reminded me of a black hole. Surrounding this was a sort of lunar rock garden, on which grew tiny plants like thymes. There were plain white walls around the garden, and projected onto these were changing images of the solar system. Naz wanted soundtracks from various science fiction films to be played as you watched the show. When you looked down from the roof garden you could see the rest of the design including a stainless steel fountain spouting coloured water into the air. Apparently it was to be accompanied by the sound of a rocket taking off from Earth. There was also an enormous flower bed using the colours of all the main planets, like orange for Mercury and Saturn, yellow for Venus and Pluto, and blue for Neptune and the Earth (though the earth looks brown and green, as well, Naz told me). This was Naz at his best.

To cut a long story short, after perusing Naz's design I felt inspired to submit a draft plan to Dr Newman, and within days he invited me to the observatory to discuss my proposal.

Naz was right, the observatory was remarkable and when I looked around I realised my initial design was too tame. I needed to liberate my imagination from all thoughts of financial limitations and practicality and let the existing building lead me into another dimension.

The road to the observatory was long and winding and passed through some desolate countryside. Then I saw a low white building ahead, and behind it a series of huge silver upturned dishes angled in the sun. I learned later that these were state of the art radio telescopes. To me they were a thing of beauty and I was mesmerised by them. The closer I got, the larger they became, until they seemed to be filling the sky. I jumped out of the car and stood for a while taking it all in.

A tall figure appeared at the door of the building. I walked towards him.

"Do you like them?" the man said.

"Yes, I do. I really do," I replied, perhaps a little too enthusiastically.

"Well, that's a promising start for someone who's hoping for a contract. You must be Josh," he said. "I'm Jacob Newman. Welcome."

We shook hands, then he beckoned me towards the open door. When Josh asked me later what I thought of Dr Newman I couldn't remember anything about his appearance, but I was struck by how relaxed he was and how passionate about his subject. He talked non-stop about the observatory and the functions of the different radio telescopes. I was lost, really, but fascinated at the same time.

When we sat down in a quiet corner, he phoned for some coffee and I had the opportunity to take in the beauty of the surroundings. I loved the simplicity of the exterior of the white building. It was very different from the observatories I was more familiar with, like Greenwich.

When we entered I hadn't expected the interior to be so aesthetically pleasing. Whilst the outside had strong linear and vertical features, the room we entered was dome shaped with a vaulted ceiling and big windows allowing light to flood in. There was an ornate spiral staircase at one end leading up to a balcony. It had a futuristic look about it. All the spaces were painted unusual muted colours and the furniture was very simple with elegant curves. In contrast there were original textile wall hangings depicting stars and planets. To me this had more in common with an art gallery than an astronomical observatory.

On reflection, I thought maybe I could adapt my design to fulfil Dr Newman's wishes. Having examined my submission he was keen to hear my ideas and listened attentively.

At the end he said, "So you're suggesting an improved visitor route via a helical staircase, leading up to a new tall tower. In the tower you want to put a sort of cultural village with galleries for interactive education, a cafe and shop. The tower is to be dome shaped, like this room, and have the appearance of a crystal with a roll top roof. You want rotating turrets within which there will be telescopes for visitors to enjoy. You've also made provisions for any visitors with mobility issues and there is to be solar heating. Excellent. Have I got that right, Josh?"

I was astonished at his grasp of my plan and his ability to summarise so concisely something which I thought was rather complex. I was a little nervous about the reaction of this highly intelligent man but I needn't have worried.

"I'll have to run it past my board, Josh, but to be honest your submission is first rate and one of the better ones. So well done. Thank you. Now how about a spot of lunch?"

I was surprised by the hospitality shown by one so famous in his field. When we entered the small dining room he said, "Do take a seat over there and then I want to introduce you to someone."

I was intrigued when he went into what looked like the kitchen and emerged followed by a young woman.

"I'd like you to meet my daughter, Carmel. Carmel, this is Josh Greenhill, Naz's equally talented brother."

Naz was right, Dr Newman's daughter was stunning and the fact that she used a wheelchair was insignificant. Naz had omitted this detail when he said how gorgeous she was. It was her hair that attracted me first. It was long and very glossy and a colour not dissimilar to my mother's, but paler.

Over lunch Dr Newman wanted to discuss how Naz and I would liase to ensure compatibility between the architecture and the landscaping. It was clear that this was no free lunch and I became aware that this man probably only stopped working when he was asleep. Even then he probably dreamed of galaxies and black holes.

When I left the observatory and drove home I was conscious of feeling excited by the prospect of working for Dr Newman on a project which was totally new ground for me. Usually, I had a faint feeling of anticipation when I was about to start a new job, but nothing like this. This was more like a Naz reaction, and it made me laugh to think of it. I was almost certain that I would be offered the contract and started to do some mental planning whilst listening to Nirvana on Rock FM.

CHAPTER ELEVEN

JOSH

The letter, when it came, was contained within a long cream envelope with an official looking crest on it, which proved to be the logo for Dr Newman's observatory. I couldn't wait to open it, I was so sure that the job was mine. When I read the first sentence and saw the word regret, I knew immediately that I was mistaken. Sure enough, Dr Newman thanked me for my excellent submission but said the competition was very strong and he regretted to tell me that the board had decided to offer the job to someone else. He urged me to contact him if I had any questions. That was it.

Hana had left for work, so I sat in silence pondering the news. Of course I'd failed to get some contracts in the past, but this was different. The fact that my twin had succeeded where I had not seemed to upset me more than I cared to admit. I had been genuinely keen to get this job as it would have been a new venture, and Dr Newman had been very impressive.

I started to get really angry when I thought about how Dr Newman had misled me into assuming I had the job but for the formality of the board discussing it. I can't believe what I did next. I took my breakfast coffee cup and threw it with all my strength at the wall. It smashed into many tiny pieces and the few dregs of coffee made a long narrow stain down the sage green paintwork. I rushed across immediately to wipe off the stain, and in so doing, I tripped and fell to the floor, hitting my head on the corner of the table. I lay there for a while, feeling dazed and a little sick. Next minute I heard a key in the door and in walked Sheila, our cleaner.

She gasped and said, "Oh, Mr Greenhill. Whatever's happened? Are you alright?"

She put her arm underneath me and with her considerable strength, for she was what is known as a buxom woman, she helped me rise.

"Thanks Sheila," I said. "I'm afraid I tripped and fell. I was carrying the coffee cup and that smashed and left a bit of a stain on the wall," I added apologetically.

"Don't worry about that, I'll clean it all up. Now you sit down and I'll make you some more coffee."

"No, that's alright. I'm fine now and I need to get off to work. Thanks again, and sorry to be a pain."

I really did feel pathetic and was glad of the drive to work to compose myself.

It seemed strange, not seeing Naz in the office. He usually popped in first thing before going off on a job. He was loving his new contract and was flourishing. I knew he should have branched off on his own years ago, and now he had I felt unusually bereft. When I returned home that evening I had to break the news to Hana. Her reaction was typically sensible.

"I'm sorry Josh, but you've plenty of interesting work lined up and I expect the board of the observatory would have queried the wisdom of employing two brothers. Might be misconstrued as favouritism." She had a slight Japanese/American accent but was word perfect.

As soon as she said that, I felt better, in a way. Of course that would be the reason. It was unlikely they would have rejected my proposal otherwise. However, as I considered this possibility further, I began to feel animosity towards my brother. If it wasn't for Naz I would have succeeded. When I look back I hate myself for my irrationality at this time. When I saw a psychotherapist months later, I began to realise that my overreaction and what happened afterwards was triggered by the death of my father. Unlike Naz I had never properly grieved and I was concealing a lot of anger at my father's sudden disappearance.

After this I carried on as normal both at home and at work, but I found myself drinking heavily and secretly. Whenever Hana was out I reached for the whisky bottle and drank until I passed out in bed. I must have been crazy to think Hana would not guess. The mornings after, I was full of regret and could not believe I had stooped so low because of a failed job application.

Around this time my mother called to say she was going away for a few days to visit a friend and could Naz and I keep an eye on the house.

I said, "Yeah, sure Mum.... I'll mention it to Naz, but he's a bit short of space now with all the travelling to Cambridge."

"Yes, I know, so whatever you think. It's only a long weekend so I'll be back Monday."

"That's fine, Mum. Anyway, you have a great time. You need to have a break."

As soon as I put down the phone my first thought was to get to my mother's house before Naz and find the photograph she had been talking to in my father's studio. I stopped short, amazed that this occurrence was still on my mind. Try as I might I could not lose the idea that I had to satisfy my curiosity. I felt as if the bit of my psyche which resembled Naz's was taking me over. At the same time I imagined that Naz was becoming more like the old me as his confidence increased through his new project. I was bewildered by it all, but determined to investigate the photograph business before I attended to my neuroticism.

I telephoned Naz that evening to pass on the news about our mother going away and assured him that he needn't worry about her house, as I would call the following day. He seemed relieved.

"Thanks for that, Josh. I've actually got a date tomorrow."

"Oh, good for you," I said. "Who's the lucky girl?"

"Well, you met Dr Newman's gorgeous daughter... believe it or not she's agreed to go out with me. We're going to the River Bar for lunch and then a walk in the Botanic Gardens."

I was astonished but tried not to show it. When Naz referred to a walk I assumed he meant he would accompany Carmel in her wheelchair.

"That's brilliant, Naz... well, have a lovely day and give my regards to Carmel. I'll speak to you on Sunday."

The photograph incident had obviously disappeared from Naz's mind despite his initial agitation. This made me wonder if I was making too much of it myself, and whether I should forget it also, but this was not in my nature. I had to resolve the mystery.

So, the following day I told Hana I needed to pop over to Mum's briefly to water her plants.

"Shall I come with you?" she said. "We could call at the pub on the way back."

"No, I'll only be about half an hour, then I thought we could try that new sushi bar in Soho."

How easy it was to conceal my real intentions. I couldn't wait to get there and, on arrival, I jumped out of the car and dashed for the door, key in hand. I fiddled to get the key in the lock (it was always awkward) and once inside I ran up the stairs. The door to my father's studio was closed and it crossed my mind that it could be locked. I panicked a bit but when I tried it the door opened wide. The portmanteau was still sitting in a corner of the room. Apart from that, the room was empty. It made me feel really sad and for the first time since the news of my father's death I was overcome with emotion. My sobs seemed to echo in the big deserted room but after about a minute I felt calmer and, wiping my eyes, I knelt by the portmanteau. When I opened it I was surprised to find it full. In spite of my mother's efforts to dispose of stuff she clearly had not been able to part with the contents of the portmanteau. I began to sift through and attempted not to get distracted by the papers and old sketches which filled the case. There were a few books, mainly poetry and art, and I shook them gently to check if the photograph was concealed within. In one of the books entitled *Art and Architecture,* there was a small drawing which interested me. The subject was a young man standing in front of an ancient domed church. At the bottom of the picture I could read 'Leon. San Angelo 1972'. It was signed by my father. I found it strangely appealing and was tempted to take it but decided not to, as my mother was obviously fond of it.

My search continued until I came across a large battered music book. I opened it carefully, sensing that my quest might be fulfilled. Sure enough, in the middle of the book was a faded photograph. I was almost afraid to look at it. But look I did, and almost fell backwards with shock.

Despite the fact that the old photograph was a little indistinct I recognised a younger Dr Newman immediately. I turned over the photo and there was his name. "To Lara from Jacob Newman with love". I couldn't have been more surprised.

"Of course!" I said to myself, remembering what Naz had told me about my mother addressing the photograph. "Jake must be short for Jacob."

This was the last thing I had expected and I was conscious of a surge of rage welling up inside me. No, worse than rage, it was more like a frenzy of madness. I threw the music book at the wall and the binding came loose, allowing all the pages to fall out and scatter on the floor. I was about to tear up the photograph but stopped myself, realising that if I was to confront my mother I might need it as evidence. There was such a muddle of thoughts going through my mind. Was it a coincidence that Dr Newman had chosen Naz for the landscaping project and invited me to tender as well? It seemed pretty unlikely and I was left thinking that he had sought us out. Maybe he was having a belated attack of conscience, having corrupted my mother and insulted my father.

When I look back I believe my behaviour at that time was abhorrent and my only defence is that the balance of my mind was upset by the unexplained death of my beloved father. Having found the photograph I left my mother's house, determined to challenge her but also to find a way of punishing Jacob Newman.

"Josh, are you alright?" Hana said when I returned home. "You look very pale, darling." She came over and pulled me to her. She was tiny next to me and her hair smelled of blossom as I towered above her. I was straight away reminded of my visit to Japan when we had fallen in love. I was close to tears again and turned my head away until I was able to speak.

"I was sorting through a few of my father's things and it all came flooding back. I suddenly felt really sad. I guess I never grieved properly at the time... always tried to be strong for my mother and Naz. The whole affair of Dad's unexplained death has hit me now, but I'm sure I'll find a way to deal with it with your help."

I still couldn't tell Hana about the photo issue because I knew she would try to dissuade me from taking any further action.

After the weekend, I returned to work as normal and kept a tight lid on my emotions. My outward composure belied the seething anger and sense of loss within. That evening my mother phoned to thank me for looking after the house.

"Was everything OK?" she asked. I wondered if she had spotted anything amiss in the studio, although I had meticulously tidied the mess and replaced the photograph.

"Yes, no problems at all. I gave the plants a drop of water but that's all that was needed. How was your weekend?"

We chatted for a while and as soon as we'd finished Naz phoned. I was unprepared but decided to keep my discovery a secret for the time being. He was very animated on the phone and full of enthusiasm for the day he'd spent with Carmel Newman.

"We're going to the theatre tomorrow night. Wondered if you and Hana wanted to join us? It's a production of Alan Aykbourn's *The Things We Do for Love* at the Arts Theatre That's if you don't mind sitting at the front with the wheelchair spaces."

"Well, we are free tomorrow and I'm sure Hana would love to meet Carmel, so I'll say, yes.'"

I wasn't sure about the wisdom of joining Naz and Carmel given my present mood, but it would have been out of character for me to refuse.

I arranged for us to meet Naz and Carmel in the cosy theatre foyer for a drink before the play.

They were deep in conversation and I noticed how Carmel never took her eyes off Naz, almost as if she were looking into his soul. She had coiled up her lovely hair onto her head and was wearing a long, almost sheer dress in pale lilac. This was one of my mother's favourite colours as it complimented her chestnut hair. When Naz caught sight of us he jumped up and waved. Carmel smiled and raised her hand in a friendly gesture. The introductions over, Hana and Carmel chatted like old friends and Naz updated me eagerly on his work project with Dr Jacob Newman.

As he was talking, I overheard Hana say something about "born in January". I was curious but just at that moment people started to get up and drift towards the auditorium, so I decided to wait until later to ask what they had talked about.

After the play we said our goodbyes and Carmel said she hoped to see us again soon. On the journey home Hana and I discussed the play. The evening out had done us good and I felt a lot more relaxed. Once home I settled down with a whisky and Hana had her usual dry white wine.

"So, you got on well with Carmel? She's really nice, isn't she?" I said.

"Yes. We have a lot in common and she seems very fond of Naz. He's certainly more at ease with himself and the world, isn't he?"

"Yes, he is." I hesitated then said, "What was it you were saying to her about "born in January"? You weren't discussing Naz's birthday were you?"

"Well, as a matter of fact, I was. Carmel mentioned that she's planning a big birthday party in January and she wants us all to go. Isn't that sweet of her, given that she's only just met us? Anyway, I said what a coincidence, the twins have birthdays in January, too. She suggested you can all celebrate together."

I sat quiet for a while. My heart was pounding and my brow was moist with perspiration. I almost dropped my whisky glass as my hand shook suddenly. My imagination, usually only active when designing buildings, was now working overtime. What was happening to me? Naz was the twin with the fertile imagination who often made mountains out of molehills.

After a while I collected my thoughts and said, "Did Carmel say what date her birthday is?"

"No. We didn't really have time to discuss details but I'm sure she'll let us know." She hesitated then said, "Are you alright Josh? You don't look yourself at all."

"Yes, I'm fine, love. Just a bit tired, that's all. Overdoing it, I expect."

"Well, I'm off to bed now. Don't be too long. You need a good night's sleep," she said as she put her hands gently on my shoulders and kissed the top of my head.

"I'll just finish my drink, then I'll be up, sweetheart."

I actually sat for another hour and finished half a bottle of whisky. The more I drank the more convinced I was that Carmel Newman was the third child to which my mother had referred, but not only that, she was also our triplet. So distressed was I by the implications, that I was on the verge of driving over to see Naz to tell him his relationship with Carmel must end at once. I got up and paced the room, wondering whether to tell Hana, to get her opinion on the best way forward. On reflection, if I had it would have saved a lot of the torment that followed.

I sat down again and drank some more whisky. I realised that driving was out of the question as I was quite drunk by now.

"This is the sort of far-fetched thing that happens on telly programmes," I said to myself. "It can't be true. But I need to find out for Naz's sake."

I asked myself whether I might be suffering from delusions. I knew this occasionally happened to people who had suffered bereavement. Then I made a decision. I must phone Naz and determine the seriousness of his relationship with Carmel. I fumbled for my mobile and despite the alcoholic haze I managed to get Naz's number. I had no idea of the time, but Naz went to bed late, being a poor sleeper, so it was likely he would still be up.

Sure enough, he answered the phone. "Josh? Is that you, mate? Are you OK?"

"Yeah... Just wanted to thank you for tonight. We both really enjoyed the evening." I was conscious my words were coming out a bit slurred. "Hana thinks Carmel's a lovely person. Totally suitable for you." I then went into drunken raptures enumerating Carmel's many qualities. Josh interrupted me.

"Hang on Josh. I've only just got to know her and we've only had a couple of dates." He sounded a bit alarmed.

"Oh, so no wedding bells yet?" I teased.

"Josh, we've not even had a proper kiss yet," he laughed.

"Do you like her though? She is rather gorgeous," I said, still probing.

"Well, yes of course, but as I say, it's early days. Anyway, shouldn't you be in bed? You sound a bit blotto. Are you?"

"I've had a few whiskies so I might be a bit merry. You should try it sometime! I'm off to bed now so see you soon and thanks again."

Based on that conversation with Naz I concluded that I could take my time in deciding my next steps. I firmly believed that Jacob Newman was our real father and Carmel was our triplet sister. I also believed that my mother was guilty of betraying my father. I needed to find a way to avenge him and I was reminded of that old adage "revenge is a dish best served cold". A few weeks delay would be advantageous.

Even poor old Naz couldn't escape my wrath because, indirectly, he had robbed me of a job I very much desired. I was conscious that taking revenge on my brother was not honourable, but my anger at the whole situation was so great that I could not think clearly.

I got on with my life as best I could, but I spent hours at work on the website searching for information about Dr Jacob Newman. There was plenty, and all of it complimentary. There were lots of accolades and long lists of his achievements and services to astrophysics both at home and abroad. This made me hate him more, because my "adopted father" Jack, as I now called him, had no such honours despite his considerable creative abilities, knowledge and personal charm. I looked at numerous photographs of Jacob Newman on the screen and could feel no connection to him.

As I searched the data I was hoping for some clues to any vulnerability. There was nothing relating to his career but there was one small news item referring to his charity work for young people with cerebral palsy. It did mention briefly that his motivation was drawn from the fact that his daughter suffered from this disability. I knew then that the only way to punish Jacob Newman was via his daughter. I dismissed any fanciful notions like kidnapping her and suddenly the idea came to me. It was so simple I couldn't believe I hadn't thought of it straight away. The answer was to do nothing but wait for Carmel and Naz to fall in love and get married. This would have devastating consequences for all parties, and Jack and I could enjoy our revenge.

CHAPTER TWELVE.

LARA

I never thought I would call one of my darling boys evil. But when Josh came and told me about his sin of omission, that's what I did.

"Josh Greenway, you are an evil person. I can't believe you are my son. To allow Naz and Carmel to marry whilst thinking they were brother and sister is despicable. If only you'd asked me the truth instead!"I screamed hysterically.

The conversation followed Naz and Carmel announcing their engagement at the big birthday party in January. We were all invited to Jacob Newman's stylish house. I hadn't seen much of Josh recently but Hana had been over for tea and said she was worried about him. She thought he was overworking and could be heading for some sort of breakdown. When I spoke to Josh on the phone he was always very jovial so I imagined that Hana was overreacting. She tended to be a little over-protective of Josh. True, he looked rather tense and ashen at the party, but his demeanour seemed buoyant if anything. He, Hana, Naz and Carmel had been playing croquet at the far end of the sweep of manicured lawn, bright green even in January. I could hear laughter and endless chatter.

Eventually they came inside, cheeks glowing with the cold. They were all wrapped up with an assortment of hats and gloves and big warm coats. Carmel looked particularly charming in a Cossack hat, long grey coat and soft wool scarf in aubergine. She and Naz were clearly excited about something and seemed a little apprehensive. It was then that Naz asked for quiet, and he and Carmel faced the throng.

"We would like to share some news with you all," Naz said. He paused. "Carmel and I are engaged to be married." It was not unexpected and everyone cheered with delight.

Josh rushed over and hugged Naz and Carmel after the announcement and spent the rest of the evening getting slowly drunk.

When Josh came to see me a week later it was a different matter. He usually looked so elegant in a casual sort of way, just like Jack used to. But on this occasion he was unshaven and his expensive clothes were hanging off him, making him look unkempt. I noticed then how much weight he had lost.

He dispensed with the pleasantries and sat down in his normal chair, an old black leather recliner.

"I need to talk to you," he said, staring directly at me.

I was anxious about what would come next as his manner was so serious.

I took his hand and said, "Are you ill, Josh? You would tell me, wouldn't you?"

He retrieved his hand and replied, "No of course not... Though when you hear what I've got to say you might think I'm sick in the head!"

"What are you talking about, Josh? Please get it over with. I'm sure it's not as bad as all that." I was rather alarmed and my whole body was tensing up.

Josh hesitated then said, "Mum, I know Jack isn't our real father. I know that you betrayed him with Jacob Newman and Newman is our father. I also know that there was a third child and that child is Newman's daughter Carmel." He explained about the overheard conversation in the studio. Then he stopped for a few minutes as if collecting his thoughts. He looked strained and was clutching the arms of the chair so that his knuckles were white. He was quiet for a moment then said, "So I wanted to avenge Jack and the way I decided to do it in the end was to do nothing. I assumed that Naz and Carmel would fall in love and that eventually they would have an incestuous marriage. If this happened, everyone would be punished who needed to be. Even poor Naz had to be punished, because if it wasn't for him I would have been appointed architect for the observatory."

I was astonished at the matter of fact way he recounted all this, and afraid at his callousness.

It was after he'd told me this that I called him evil. This made him very angry and he stood up and paced the room for a few seconds, clenching and unclenching his hands.

"You're the evil one," he shrieked. "I can't believe you didn't stop the engagement knowing what it would lead to. You can't think I really wanted this to happen. I just wanted to force you to be honest... But you didn't have the guts. You've hidden the truth from me and Naz all these years and you couldn't tell us even to stop a disastrous event taking place which would bring shame on us all."He was shaking with anger as he shouted at me and I feared he might turn violent.

"Naz, please sit down and I'll explain everything to you... It's not all as it seems. Why don't we have a glass of wine and then we can talk properly?"

That suggestion seemed to calm him a bit and he poured two glasses of wine then sat.

"Naz, you're right in part." I told him about my passionate long term but casual relationship with Jacob Newman, and how we had been intimate shortly before we were both due to marry other people.

"I was terrified that I might be pregnant as a result. We had been careless, having had a lot to drink, so I regret to say I seduced Jack when he was off-guard to ensure that he would appear to be the father if I found I was pregnant."

As I confessed this to Josh I had vivid recollections of the occasion when Jack and I had been walking through some woodland close by. It was very secluded and the perfect place to make love. Even now the scent of bluebells brings to mind the memory and the mix of emotions, joy and sorrow.

"Sometime later, after Jack and I were married, I found that I was expecting not one but three babies. Jack was overjoyed and I convinced myself that you were his children. The possibility that Jacob might be the father became a deeply buried secret." As I continued Josh sat quietly, listening intently. "In fact, I started to believe that Jack really was your father. He was a twin and I thought this would increase the chance of a multiple birth for me. I only started to think about it again after Jack died. The more I thought about you and Naz the more I noticed mannerisms and characteristics that reminded me of Jake. The way you walk, the way you stare people out, how you can both be stubborn and oversensitive but also your extraordinary intensity and gentleness. I have to be honest with you.... Although I loved Jack dearly, I never lost that physical desire for Jake that I'd always had. I desperately wanted to tell him about his three children but I knew it would destroy our lives. That's why Naz caught me talking to Jake's photograph. I'm deeply ashamed of that, and embarrassed. Naz has never mentioned the matter so I'm wondering if you reassured him and suggested that he'd misheard? I do hope so. It's the sort of level headed thing you would do. He's always been so vulnerable somehow."

Josh spoke at last, in a quiet and controlled way, "Yes, I did persuade Naz that he might have heard wrongly. He still seemed keen to get to the bottom of it but I suspect his relationship with Carmel put things in perspective and that he's forgotten all about it. Despite his sensitivity he seems to have the capacity to do that. Unfortunately I seem to be the opposite. When Naz first told me, I really thought you had said Jack was the father of your three children, but the fact that there was only me and Naz made me wonder. I always thought you and Jack were very loving, but more like a fond brother and sister. So the idea that your passion lay elsewhere became more of a reality." His words came tumbling out like a torrential waterfall and I struggled to keep up with all that Josh was relating.

"When I failed to get the job at the observatory Hana suggested that it was probably because the board felt they might be accused of favouritism if they appointed two brothers. After this I fell to pieces and started to drink heavily. I couldn't control my anger towards Jacob, you and Naz, hence my decision to let things slide. By not exposing your betrayal of Jack I knew there was a strong possibility Naz and Carmel would enter an incestuous marriage unless you intervened." Josh halted and sat waiting for my reaction.

Although I was appalled at Josh's handling of the situation – it was so unlike him to be this emotional and cruel – I blamed myself for not being open with both of the boys. I really respected his honesty and imagined that it had taken a lot of courage to confess. It made me feel very sad.

"Josh, I'm so sorry that my lack of honesty has led to this awful state of affairs. You must have been suffering a lot to have taken such a spiteful decision... So out of character."

I longed for my cello at this point and somewhere in my subconscience I could hear Dvorak's cello concerto. I hung onto that and also imagined that Jack was holding my hand as he had done so many times when I was in trouble.

"I have to tell you, Carmel Newman is not your sister." I took a deep breath. "The truth is, the third triplet was a girl but she died a week after birth. Hard to accept that was almost forty years ago. Not a day goes by that I don't think about it. Her name was Leonora. Jack chose it. We couldn't bring ourselves to tell you." The memory was so painful that I was close to tears and had to take some deep breaths to steady myself. Strangely, Josh seemed unconcerned.

"I see," he said. His words had a cutting edge to them. He paused then asked, "So did you know Jacob Newman was Naz's boss?"

"Well yes, of course I did. I was astonished when Naz told me and concluded that Jake had tracked you both down with a view to employing you."

"So he only took Naz on because he was your son?" Josh said, sounding outraged.

"Of course not. You would have to be truly excellent to match up to Jake's standards and I'm positive he would have been frustrated not to be able to employ you as well."

"Did you see Jacob before the birthday party?" he asked.

"No, there's been no communication between us at all. He's happily married and I still love Jack and I miss him so much. He was my tower of strength."

Josh poured us another glass of wine and we sat in silence, both lost in our own thoughts. Then Josh seemed to rouse himself and as he stood up he said, "Look Mum, I need to get back. Sorry this has been rather upsetting for you. I'll think about what you've told me and then maybe we can have another chat if that's OK?"

I was unsure how to respond as I'd expected a more positive reaction from Josh. Maybe I was too impatient. After all it must have come as a surprise, everything I'd shared with him. Yet I had an unsettling feeling that Josh had not totally believed what I'd said. Surely he didn't really think that Carmel was his triplet sister? Having said that, I must admit she and I did look a bit alike, but that was just coincidence. Josh must be able to see that.

When Josh had left I felt drained and went straight to the music room to sit for a while and play a challenging Bach piece. Gradually the tension drained away and I immersed myself in the depths of the music. I reflected on happier times when Jack first took me to Durham to the Miners' Gala and remembered how wonderful it was to be cosseted by his mother. Being at one with the music enabled me to find sanctuary in my recollections, and telling Josh the truth at last had freed me from the guilt I had carried all these years. The tranquility did not last long unfortunately. About a fortnight later the phone rang. When I answered it I was astonished to hear Jake's voice.

"Hello, Lara. How are you?" He didn't wait for an answer but went on, "I know we agreed not to meet on our own but something has happened and I need to talk to you." Jake sounded quite desperate.

I felt shaken by what he had said, trying to imagine what the problem was. It must be something to do with Naz or Josh, I surmised.

"OK. Where would you like to meet?" I said hesitantly.

"I wondered if it would be alright for me to come over to your house?" he replied.

I wasn't really sure about the wisdom of this but could think of no alternative so I agreed. We arranged to meet the next day at lunchtime.

I found it hard to sleep that night and as I tossed and turned I imagined all sorts of things that might have caused Jake to be so anxious to see me after all this time. I was glad when six a.m. arrived and I felt it was reasonable to rise. It was still dark but after coffee I sat down at my cello and played for about an hour, then decided to get dressed. I soaked in a hot fragrant bath and washed my hair with organic honeysuckle rose shampoo. I took my time choosing an outfit and decided on a mossy green knitted dress. It was only when I observed myself in the mirror that I was forced to acknowledge that I had dressed to impress.

I was expecting Jake at midday but he was late as always. He didn't apologise but instead thrust a bouquet of yellow roses in my direction. He had remembered that they were my favourite.

"Come in, Jake," I said, and led him into the conservatory. It was the brightest room in the house of course and overlooked a small garden. Well it was more of a yard, really, filled with pots of flowers inspired by Jack's mother and planted by my gardener.

"Would you like something to eat?" I desperately hoped he would decline as I was still a terrible cook and rarely had anything interesting to prepare.

"No thanks, Lara. I'm fine. We had a late breakfast this morning."

He didn't look as if he'd missed any sleep last night and, except for his greying unruly hair and what appeared to be a large bruise on his cheekbone he hardly appeared any different from years ago. I still found him very attractive.

"How are you, Lara? You're looking quite radiant," he said.

I ignored this remark, thinking how charming he still was.

"What about some coffee? I've actually got some good coffee beans... Jack's influence."

"Oh, Lara. I meant to say how very sorry I was to hear about Jack's death. You must have been devastated... and the boys too."

"Thank you. Yes, it was a terrible shock. But we're coming to terms with it now. It was a long time ago." I didn't want to discuss it any further as I couldn't guarantee I wouldn't cry, so I asked him again what he would like to drink. He opened a bag he had brought in and held up a bottle of, Dom Perignon.

"Is it too early for you?"

"No, a glass of champagne would be lovely. Thank you." I almost laughed when I recalled what had happened last time we had got drunk on champagne. We were much older now, so a passionate outcome was unlikely.

Jake had seated himself on the sofa and I sat opposite him in my favourite armchair. After a few sips of champagne I began to feel quite relaxed. Jake didn't speak for a while but held his glass between two hands and appeared to be staring right through me. I was used to this habit and simply smiled. I felt I had to break the silence, although it was very agreeable just enjoying Jake's company.

"Is there something you wanted to discuss with me, Jake?" I said.

"Yes, well, no. What I mean is I wanted to tell you about an incident that happened the day before yesterday."

I listened attentively, not knowing what to expect.

"It was about eight p.m. and I'd just returned from work when the doorbell rang. Who should be standing there but Josh."

"Josh?" I said "But what did he want?" I was bewildered.

"I'll describe exactly what happened. I said I was surprised to see him but pleased and invited him in. No sooner had I said that than he threw a left hook and hit my cheekbone hard. He was going for my nose but missed, thankfully."

I examined the bruise on Jake's face and experienced a great sense of shame and anger. I drank some more champagne to steady my nerves and listened as Jake continued.

"I was completely off guard and reeled backwards into the wall of the porch. I could feel some blood trickle down where Jake had cut my skin. I put up my fists in case of further punches but Josh bowed his head and I could see the fight had gone out of him. I asked him what the hell he was doing and he said he was sorry and could he come in and talk to me. It was deja vu."

"What do you mean, Jake?"

"Well, I'd made a promise to myself never to tell you this, but circumstances are different now, so I will."

"Tell me what?" I said, impatient to make sense of the conversation.

"Well, you may remember, many years ago, just before we both got married, I visited you at your house and the Dom Perignon proved to be a powerful aphrodisiac. Jack turned up afterwards and sensed that something had happened between us. He came to my hotel that evening and was so distressed at the idea that I might be stealing you away that he hit me in the face. He's a better fighter than young Josh... he did get my nose!" Jake laughed when he said this but I found myself unable to join in, I was so shocked at what I had heard.

"I never knew that happened. I'm so sorry. You must think we're all deranged monsters," I said. I felt very uncomfortable and took another drink whilst I tried to collect my thoughts.

"Lara, please don't give it another thought. Jack and Josh are similar. They're both full of passion and want to protect what they hold dear."

I really respected Jake for being so forgiving. "So what happened after Josh hit you?"

"Well, he came in and we sat down and drank a large Glenfiddich, each without saying a word. We both needed to compose ourselves. Josh opened the conversation by apologising, then he suddenly burst into tears and sobbed for about five minutes. I wasn't sure what to do so I just let him get on with it. This seemed to do the trick because he calmed down and then he started to talk. He told me that he had discovered that I was his and Naz's father and that Carmel was their triplet sister. I was astounded but listened in silence until he'd finished. He confessed his plan for punishing me, you and Naz. He stressed that he hadn't wanted to hurt Carmel... She was just an innocent victim. He also emphasised that he thought you would intervene and stop Carmel and Naz's relationship before it was too late. He really condemned you for not doing this." Jake paused for breath and finished his drink. He gave me that long, expectant soul searching look for which he was famous.

"What you've told me isn't news. Josh disclosed all this to me recently, and I was able to tell him that Carmel isn't his sister. I did have triplets and the third one was a girl whom we called Leonora, but sadly she died in hospital not long after birth. But I had to be honest and admit that I believed you to be his father." I waited for Jake's reaction. Had he ever suspected that this was the case?

"Lara, my love. I wish you'd told me about all this before now, and I could have put your mind at rest."

"Why, what do you mean?" I said, feeling unnerved. This wasn't the response I had anticipated.

Jake hesitated then said, "I've never broadcasted this for obvious reasons, but I'm actually infertile... I won't bore you with the details. When we found out we were so desperate for a child that Helen and I decided to adopt. That's how Carmel came into our lives. She'd been abandoned at birth and was left wrapped in a blanket inside a cardboard box outside a synagogue in Cambridge."

Jake must have noticed my look of disbelief, as he then said, "I know it's a bit of a fairy story but it's completely true, and we were the fortunate people who were chosen as her parents."

"I see. Did you explain all this to Josh?"

"Yes, of course."

"And did he seem to believe you? When I told him about Leonora dying I got the impression he thought this was a lie? I guess that's one of the reasons he came to see you... to check your version."

"Yes, I think you're probably right. I'm sure what I said put his mind at rest. When he left he certainly looked happier. He didn't mention the job issue so I suspect that has faded into the background now."

"I think I can understand Josh imagining that Carmel might be his sister. After all, she does look a bit like me, her hair being such a similar colour, and her birthday is the same as my sons'. I must admit I'm very puzzled about that."

"Let me reassure you, Lara. The hair colour is pure coincidence and I'm so glad it's like yours... I've always loved it. As for the birthday, we were informed by the Jewish adoption agency that, based on the doctor's report, they were almost sure Carmel was born in January, but as her real mother had disappeared without trace, they had no way of knowing which date. By chance, you'd sent me a card to tell me about the birth of your boys. Do you remember? So I thought it would be nice to give Carmel the same birthday. It seemed to keep us all connected. Helen thought it was a random choice and she was happy with that."

"But didn't Naz think the same as Josh?" I said.

"Not really. According to Carmel he really did think it was a happy coincidence and a good omen."

"Oh... my darling Naz... so pure and naïve."

"Yes, he's a very special young man, and so is Josh but in a different way," Jake replied.

We drank some more champagne and then Jake took his leave. There was no attempt to do anything dishonourable this time. To be honest, I was a bit sorry and knew then that all passion between Jake and me was history. I also felt strangely deflated at having learned the truth about Josh, Naz, and Carmel. I should have been relieved but believing that Jake was the boys' father had been a sort of romantic notion that gave me some comfort and helped me deal with Jack's death. I moved to the music room and set up my cello. I continued with Bach's cello suite No.1. I was a few bars in when I was suddenly overwhelmed with feelings of guilt. I realised that my life had been built on lies and deceit which I had buried deep within me. How could I have allowed that to happen? I knew that I would need to spend some time working through this to be able to come to terms with it all. I decided to see if I could go and spend a few days with Jack's mother, Audrey. She was very old now, but still managing at home with help from carers and Jack's brother. Being with her always gave me a sense of peace and the beautiful garden was an ideal place to reflect on recent events.

When I revealed to Audrey that I had done something dishonest concerning Jack and my sons, she said in that clear soft voice hardly altered by age, "Lara, I know you loved Jack, and whatever you think you did it will have been for all the right reasons. Now forget it and forgive yourself. I trust you implicitly, so trust yourself."

With this she grasped my hand and I closed my eyes and dreamed that it was Jack beside me. This time I let the tears flow freely. When I returned home I felt refreshed and indeed I had found a way to forgive myself. I hoped that Josh would be able to go through a similar catharsis with the aid of someone like Audrey.

The next time I saw Jacob was at Naz and Carmel's June wedding. After our talk, Josh decided, with Hana's support, to take a little time off work and seek counselling. He was still depressed but the main concerns were his acute anger about Jack dying without trace, and anger at himself for what he regarded as unforgivable behaviour. Once he began to feel better he and Hana went off to Japan for a month to visit my father. When he returned for Naz's wedding he looked wonderful and was back in control, but seemed to have an inner peace which had always been missing in both my sons. He shared with Naz that the psychotherapist had suggested that the death of their triplet sister may have been a factor.

Hana and I had tea together and she told me all about their trip to Japan. It was cherry blossom time and both she and Josh enjoyed this partly because it reminded them of when they first met and fell in love. She said my father was amazing. He was clearly shocked when he met them at the airport and saw how thin and ill Josh looked.

He said, "You've obviously been in the wars Josh. Don't tell me the details but we'll see if we can make you smile again."

The month that followed was filled with relaxing activities and health giving food.

"We spent a week at one of the volcanic hot springs resorts in Hakone. It has a wonderful view of Mount Fuji. I wish you could see it... and the whole experience makes you feel so good physically and mentally. All your stresses melt away," Hana said. "I was so relieved to see Josh coming back to life and he's not just the same as he was, but better. I can't thank your father and Karin enough." At this point she looked a little coy and then she said, "By the way, we have some good news."

"Oh yes, what is it Hana?" I thought I could guess and I was right.

"We're expecting a baby... well actually, two babies!"

So by the time Naz and Carmel's wedding came around I was feeling restored and looking forward to the celebration. The wedding was not a traditional Jewish affair in the synagogue. Jacob and Helen were what I think is described as secular Jews, and they had raised Carmel accordingly, so there was no question of Naz having to convert. Thus they decided to have both the marriage ceremony and the banquet at the observatory. I was very excited about seeing the grounds which Naz had designed and also the internal improvements. I hoped Josh would keep his cool and allow his brother a perfect day.

I got to the observatory early on the day of the wedding as Naz and Carmel had asked if I would play some cello music with my quartet during the ceremony, and we wanted to practice. We were to play Pachelbel's *Canon* whilst everyone was finding a seat, followed by Wagner's *Wedding March* as Carmel approached the front. I made a promise to myself to return at some future date to explore properly, and proceeded to the observatory.

The room where the ceremony was to be held was the first one you came to on entering the observatory. The observatory itself was rather stark, with no elegant curves, just lots of straight lines at different levels. But once inside I loved the wedding room for its dome shaped ceiling and huge windows which filled the place with light. I also liked the use of bright, textile hangings and unusual colour schemes. I touched the hangings gently and was fascinated to find they depicted all kinds of planets and stars. There were intimate spaces for sitting and a beautiful spiral staircase. I couldn't help thinking Jack would have approved.

At last the wedding ceremony was to start. I was always a little on edge before an important engagement even after all these years. When Carmel entered I found it difficult to continue for she was walking with great effort using one stick with her left hand and linking Jake's arm with the other. Jake was carrying her bouquet with his free hand. The bouquet was a beautiful sight with fragrant peach and lavender roses and a few sparkling crystal droplets cascading from it. It took Carmel a while to reach the front so we played the piece twice. The room was exceedingly quiet and, although everyone kept their eyes forward, I think we were all conscious of a little miracle taking place. I'm sure most people were blinking back tears and when Carmel reached Naz, she turned round and smiled with elation. Suddenly someone started to clap and then there was rapturous applause.

When it subsided she said, "Yes, Lara and her quartet were rather good, weren't they?"

So typical of Carmel. How we all adored her, most of all Naz, who grasped her hands and kissed them gently, supporting her all the while. They stood together arms linked beneath an archway of flowers. Carmel looked enchanting in her creamy white, lace vintage wedding gown, and Naz was as handsome as can be. Jacob stood back, taking care of the bouquet and also Carmel's wheelchair which was looking very festive decorated with tiny rosebuds and silk ribbons. Josh, the best man, also stood aside. Seeing Jacob, Josh and Naz in close proximity I was left in no doubt that they were not related by blood but only by my love for them all.

Just as the ceremony was to begin the door opened and a few stragglers came in. There was standing room only by then so they gathered at the back. I didn't take any notice of them, although one person did stand out a bit. He was a thin elderly man with dark glasses and thick grey hair. There was something about his distinguished appearance which interested me. I thought he might be from abroad as he was quite tanned. He was wearing a black leather jacket and immaculate white shirt but no tie. He didn't seem to be dressed for a wedding but I guessed he must be a friend of Carmel's family. Anyway, I forgot about him as the registrar started to speak. I have to say it was a very special wedding and throughout Naz and Carmel only had eyes for each other. They seemed to be in a blissful world of their own making. Maybe it was special because of the presence of so many people I loved. My father and Karin had flown over, Josh and Hana were there and Jack's mother had been escorted down by Jack's brother. My dear friend Felice was there, too. The only people missing were my darling Jack and Jake's father who had died several years earlier.

When the ceremony was over and Naz pushed Carmel in her wheelchair towards the sunshine, I played my heart out. It was a favourite piece of the quartet's, *The Finale* from Handel's Water Music. As the guests began to follow, we changed the tempo a bit and played a medley of Beatles tunes much to everyone's delight. There was *Here Comes The Sun*, *All My Loving*, *She Loves You* and a few others.

To my surprise this gave rise to an impromptu dance when all Naz's and Carmel's friends encircled them and began to move spontaneously in time to the music. Gradually everyone joined in, singing along. Suddenly there was a vast panorama of stars being projected onto the walls and ceiling. The whole scene was euphoric and I was very moved. I thought this must be a new chapter in our lives.

There were to be some photographs in the grounds so I wanted to secure my cello in the car beforehand. I was on my way to the car park when I noticed the distinguished latecomer photographing Naz and Carmel using a telephoto lens. As I crossed the car park he panned across the grounds, obviously taking some general scenes including some of me. I wondered what this stranger would think when he looked at the photographs. There I was, still commanding attention with my tall stature and flame coloured hair. I had aged, of course, but being a performer I had learned to hide it well. I placed my cello in the back of my Peugot and when I returned to the crowds the man had disappeared.

Suddenly I heard the roar of an expensive motorbike and saw it skid to a halt. I recognised it as a Ducati. Jack had bought one similar after we were married, although it was a Yamaha that took him to his death. I heard the rider calling in what sounded like Italian and the distinguished man in dark glasses appeared and called back. I have a basic knowledge of Italian for my music and thought he said *"Ciao. Che pracere vederti"*.

He went across and they embraced warmly, then he put on a crash helmet and mounted. The two rode off at great speed and I was left to my musings as I watched them disappear beyond the horizon. Out of nowhere my two boys appeared. They each linked one of my arms, manoevring me gently towards the photographer and other guests.

"What were you smiling at Mum?" said Naz, looking at me quizzically.

"Oh nothing really... just memories and this beautiful day. If only your father could have been here."

Acknowledgements

Thanks to David York, of Sheffield, for agreeing to let me use his beautiful photograph of a cellist sculpture, which can be found in the wonderful gardens of Renishaw Hall.

Robert Frost (1874 – 1963) (Chapter Nine)

An American poet, highly regarded for his realistic depiction of rural life. *The Road Not Taken* is one of his best known poems.

The Garden of Cosmic Speculation (Chapter Ten)

Charles Jencks and his wife Maggie Keswick conceived this unique garden in 1989. It has been evolving ever since. Charles Jencks (born 1939) is an American architectural theorist, landscape architect and designer, and co-founder of Maggie's Cancer Care Centres.